CHARLEE JAMES

EVERNIGHT PUBLISHING ®

www.evernightpublishing.com

CHARLEE JAMES

DEDICATION

For Kelsy
So good to have you home

CHARLEE JAMES

VISION OF POWER

Vision Series, 2

Charlee James

Copyright © 2022

Prologue

Cold. Cold and fear and pain. These were her constant companions since she'd been taken. The dirt floor beneath her bare bottom was the softest surface in the basement. She wouldn't go near the stained mattress. Not without kicking and screaming. Yesterday, the sound of a police siren brought such a wave of promise, of hope. Then the man had laughed as tears blurred in her eyes. The sound had faded. No one was coming for her. Were they even looking?

"They won't remember you, Janie. This is your life now. Until I say otherwise."

Her stomach recoiled at the sound of his voice, high-pitched and shrill. The tone of it iced her insides.

"Stop calling me that!" The scream ripped from her throat. "My name is Kinley Miller!"

Blinding pain erupted as the man's fist connected with her cheek. A sickening crack of bone. Stars danced behind her lids.

"Get on the mattress." His voice was calm now,

almost amused, and fear rippled through her. "I'm gonna teach you a lesson, Janie."

Her bladder loosened with terror. "No, no, no."

"No!" Kinley shot up in bed, the sheets twining around her ankles like shackles. That was the first indication she was in her bedroom, in the safety of her apartment. A sarcastic chuff broke from her lips. Security was just a façade, one that had been shattered for her long ago. She kicked off the sheets and wrapped her fingers around the Glock holstered to the side of her nightstand. The weight of the heavy polymer frame slowed the rapid boom of her heart. She wasn't a defenseless child, but a homicide detective with the Massachusetts State Police Department. Not a day went by when she didn't think of her captor—the man who single-handedly changed the trajectory of her life. Fifteen victims had died at his hands. One lived to escape—her. These days, it was more a curse than a blessing. The worst part? He'd evaded capture. The case was cold.

She peered at her cell phone. Three o'clock in the morning. What a way to start the day. There was no going back to sleep now, so she swung her legs over the side of the bed and stalked toward the bathroom, flipping on the lights as she went. The nightmares were nothing new, but they had increased in intensity, most likely born from stress on the job. It had been a hell of a few months for the homicide department, ending when the main suspect of a string of murders abducted Detective Gus Lambert's love interest and held her at gunpoint. Lambert was her friend and one of the finest detectives she'd ever had the pleasure of working alongside.

Kinley hadn't hesitated to take out the perpetrator holding Lambert's girlfriend. After pulling the trigger, she'd gone through the department's psych evaluation and had been cleared to return to duty. Burying herself in work was the best way to forget about her unresolved issues. She scrubbed her hands over her face, not sparing a glance in the bathroom mirror, and cranked on the hot water. After shedding her clothes, she stepped beneath the scalding spray. She washed quickly, trying to ignore the ridges and dents of old scars that marred her skin. Each was a reminder that she'd bested the beast who put them there.

She reached out of the shower, fumbling for a towel, and knotted it above her breasts. The illuminated screen of her cell phone made her take pause. She took two careful steps across the tile, slick with steam from her shower, and peered at the screen. It wouldn't be a Monday morning without emails flooding her inbox. She scrolled through, thumb freezing on a one-word subject line.

Janie. That one word, that one name, was the pull of a trigger, and her heart flew out of the barrel, rocketing faster than the speed of sound. She drew in a breath through her nose, trying to quell the growing panic pushing down on her sternum. Static roared in her ears as she fumbled to open the cabinet below the sink, reaching for her security blanket. The Sig Sauer might not be soft and fuzzy, but it damn well served the same purpose. Some might call her paranoid. She called it prepared. Towel still sheathed around her, Kinley raced into the bedroom, checking the locks on windows and doors in every room in the apartment. The deadbolts were engaged. The windows locked uptight. Chest heaving, she returned to her room and sat in the middle of her bed.

Subject: Janie

She stared at the email. A metallic taste rose in her throat, coating her tongue. Maybe it was nothing.

Maybe it was everything she'd been expecting since the day she turned eighteen and left Kansas. She'd climbed out the dank basement window, the sting of broken glass tugging the skin of her belly and wrists as she struggled, and had known this day would come. The man who had taken her innocence, her sense of safety, and every scrap of dignity she ever possessed would come for her, whether it took five minutes, a decade, or longer.

"Kinley," she whispered through gritted teeth. "My name is Kinley."

Chapter One

"Thanks for meeting me." Kinley sat with her back to the wall, a ceramic coffee mug warming her palms. The scents of bacon grease and frying potatoes coated the air. When she finally worked up the courage to open the email last night, she was thrust back into a nightmare. In a moment of panic, she called on her friend and fellow detective's brother, who was some kind of cybersecurity savant for the FBI. The bureau's field office wasn't too far from the state police barracks. Easton Adair had agreed to the early six o'clock meeting without hesitation.

"Don't thank me." Easton slid next to her on the bench. Neither of them would feel comfortable with their back to the room. "After what you did for my brother and his fiancée, you're part of our misfit family whether you want to be or not."

Her cheeks heated, and she redirected her eyes to the interior of her coffee cup. Being thanked for doing her job, doing what Gus Lambert would've done for her in a heartbeat, made her uncomfortable.

"Even if you hadn't been able to do what you did that day, I'd still be here." His dark eyes reflected the sincerity riding the low timbre of his voice.

"Why?" He didn't know her, had no reason to do her any favors despite the fact she was as close to partners as it got with Easton's brother. "Gus has only introduced us in passing."

Easton angled his body slightly toward her, his face unreadable. "Maybe I feel a sort of kinship with you. Gus told me … some of what you've lived through. No personal details, just who and where."

Her heartbeat echoed in her ears. Gus hadn't told

her what Easton had been through, only that they'd met in foster care.

"You were taken?" She set her coffee mug down. There was a flash of pain, along with something more—something that looked like fury in his eyes.

"No. I used to pray to be, though." He didn't flinch as he said the words, but she could hear the unbridled truth behind each syllable. She wanted to ask him more but didn't want to dredge up bad memories, and if she wasn't mistaken, their server was headed straight for their table holding a freshly brewed pot of coffee.

A middle-aged man extended his arm. "Coffee?" he said, angling his chin toward Easton.

"Yes, please." He tipped over the upside-down mug. Bitter steam plumed up as the scalding liquid splashed against ceramic. She stole a glance at Easton while he averted his attention to the waiter. Unlike her light-brown irises, his were rich and dark like glossed mahogany, framed by black-rimmed glasses. His hair was the same dark brown, and a bit mussed like he'd rolled out of bed and swept his fingers through it before leaving the house. Short, but a bit longer on top of his head. He looked like a scruffier Clark Kent—edgier. More dangerous. Just more.

When the waiter walked away with their breakfast order, Easton's attention quickly snapped back to her. "Tell me." His words were more demand than a question. He poured creamer and three sugar packets into his cup, stirred, and replaced the spoon on his napkin.

"I had a nightmare. It woke me, so I got up, took a shower, and scrolled through my email." She plucked her phone from the purse sitting at her outer thigh, found what she was looking for, and offered it to him. "This was in my inbox." If he noticed the tremor in her hands, he didn't say anything about it. She was grateful for that, hating to be in a position of weakness.

"Janie—we're not so different now, are we?" he read in a hushed tone. The words lost some of their menace spoken through Easton's voice. When she'd recited them in her head, it was as though the Kingston Town Killer, as the media had dubbed him, had spoken them. His terrible, squeaky voice panting in her ear. Janie. Janie. Janie. Attached to the email was a picture of her leaving the scene of Sasha's abduction. The one where she'd used deadly force to take down the perpetrator.

"When I was thirteen, I was abducted from a shopping center." She took a sip of her coffee to ease some of the tightness in her throat, but the acidic beverage only made her gut twist more. "After two months, I saw a chance to escape, and I took it. I knew my time was running out." She took a deep breath, then continued. "There were other victims. The basement I was held in showed signs of frequent use. Dried blood, a stained, dirty mattress. Clumps of hair here and there."

Easton studied her over the rim of his mug, intently listening. He said nothing at all, showed no shock or disgust, so she continued. "He'd carelessly left a hammer on the floor after one of his torture sessions. There was this square cutout in the concrete dividing two sides of the basement. I was able to climb in and take the nails out of a boarded window on the other side. It wasn't until a few days after I was rescued that investigators told me how many victims he'd actually had." After telling her story to law enforcement and the FBI hundreds of times, she could reiterate her experience almost clinically.

"We studied the Kingston Town Killer at the academy in Quantico. Fifteen bodies. Some identified, and some remains that are still unknown today. One partial fingerprint. One survivor. Kinley Miller. You were brave enough to save yourself. To hang in long enough to do that." His gaze was locked on her face. Instead of squirming beneath his intense stare, though, the weight on her shoulders dissipated a fraction. She never relied on anyone for anything, but here was Easton, offering acceptance and understanding. That made him different from anyone she'd known before. "Why did you decide to change your last name?"

"The case was everywhere. For a long time, I couldn't turn on the television or look at a paper that didn't have my face plastered on it. I took my mother's maiden name when I got older so I could blend in. Be harder to find. Not just from the media and true crime fanatics, but from him." A long breath involuntarily shuddered from her lungs.

"A name can be a blessing or a curse." His jaw clenched, then relaxed. "It was a smart detail to change. If he were looking, it would take him some time to discover you."

She nodded. "I always wondered if he'd moved on and kept killing in another location, or if he was biding his time to finish me first."

His Adam's apple bobbed as he took a long drink of coffee and then placed the mug down with a click. "You told the agents working your case that he called you Janie throughout your time in captivity, but it's a classified detail. Are there any other civilians who know that information? Who might slip it into an email to scare you, to punish you in some way? Maybe an angry ex, a friend you had a falling out with?"

The tips of her hair brushed her neck as she shook her head. "Not—not even my parents." She stammered. "I didn't want them to sit in on the interviews. Even at thirteen, I got that it wasn't my fault that I was raped and tortured. They would've loved me regardless of what he'd done, but a little part of me always wondered if it would be less. If I was less. I don't know."

"No one wants to be seen as the broken, tainted thing. Everyone thinks they know the best ways to piece you back together. The right glue to seal up the cracks without understanding that nothing fits back into place once it's been shattered."

The deep roll of his voice soothed her. To this day, a high-pitched male voice sent shivers coursing down her spine.

She was torn between relief at being understood and tightness in her chest—pain that he'd endured something extraordinarily terrible, as well. They paused again as the waiter dropped off their French toast and pancakes. They both ignored the food and picked up on their conversation.

"What do you think the sender means?" His voice dropped an octave, and he leaned in closer. The scent of him surprised her—sweet, homey—maybe amber or a hint of patchouli. Calming. "We're not so different now?"

"I had just killed the man who abducted Sasha. The media had taken some photographs that captured other officers and me leaving the woods. A few articles came out in the local paper. I can't recall a closeup of myself, but I suppose someone could've cropped a picture." Imagining other scenarios had goosebumps coursing down her arms.

"I'll compare all of the photographs taken at the scene. We need to find out who had access to those files, or if someone else we don't know about was there that day." He moved his plate closer, then hers. "Eat. You'll feel steadier after."

She wasn't sure what to make of him telling her what to do. The typical reaction certainly wasn't the warmth currently ballooning in her chest. She cut into her pancakes. It had been years since someone had cared enough to boss her around, mainly because she didn't let anyone outside of her fellow officers get close.

"So," he said after a few moments. "You've taken a life. He's taken several lives. In a twisted way, it brings you down to his level. If the killer sent this to you, maybe he's been waiting for something of significance, some sign, that he should contact you. You're not an innocent anymore in his eyes, even though you had to make a difficult decision to save innocent lives while his actions are predatory, about gaining power over his victims."

"You think it's him?" The girl inside her trembled right down to her soul, while the detective perked up with a twinge of excitement. What if he could be caught? It would mean so much to so many. Broken families to have justice for their loved ones. For her, it would mean a chance to look into the sick bastard's eyes and ask him why. Once he was locked away, she wouldn't let her guard down, but it would be one less shadow lurking at her back.

"I think we need to proceed with caution and assume the email was a threat. Once we can uncover the IP address that sent the correspondence, we might have the first solid lead in over a decade." He flipped his hand over on the table, offering it to her. After a moment of hesitation, she slipped her palm into his much larger one. The gesture wasn't meant to be anything remotely sexual, but suddenly, her fingers were the source of a million tiny nerve receptors, all firing off at once, transmitting tingles up her arms. His posture suddenly went rigid, and his lips parted. Had he felt it too? That flare of chemistry, like an accelerant-fueled blaze?

He released her hand, reaching for his coffee cup right away. "Thank you for trusting me with this." His voice sounded thicker than it had before. "I'll notify my supervisor and start seeing if I can get a handle on the sender's digital footprint. Based on the killer's profile, he'd be pushing mid-sixties or early seventies right now. Maybe we'll luck out and he won't be as tech-savvy as someone born with a tablet in their hands."

"Maybe he's finally slipped up." The question on her mind was if they would find him before he could find her.

Chapter Two

Habit had Easton surveying the parking lot before he stepped out of the diner with Kinley. The fine hairs on the back of his neck stood, making him take pause. He didn't like the unease squirming beneath his skin, the aura of being watched. He kept his hand just behind the small of her back, never touching, just hovering there in case they had to move fast. Outwardly, Kinley's movements were loose and relaxed as they crossed the parking lot, but her eyes gave her away—liquid gold. Scanning. Assessing. Everything about her had a gilded glow: her hair, the dusting of freckles over the bridge of her nose. But her spine? That was made of steel. Thick gray clouds billowed in tufts across the sky, making the temperature seem ten degrees colder than a typical fall day.

"Humor me." He stopped halfway across the parking lot. "Use your automatic start."

Her brows winged up, but she pressed the button on her key fob. The car started without incident. Maybe he was overly cautious, but an explosive had been placed beneath his brother's car a few months ago. He could've been gravely injured, but he'd come away with only a few scrapes.

"You're not going to start treating me like a civilian, right? Telling me to be careful and to lock up at night?" Her dry tone made him want to chuckle, despite the severity of the situation. The urge to laugh wasn't something that happened often. He didn't try to let go of the nightmare of his past. It was part of who he was and why he'd chosen a career with the bureau. To rid the world of monsters—especially those who lurked behind familiar names and faces. Mother. Father. Uncle. Coach.

"During the day, too." He gave Kinley a small smile to let her know he was joking. He respected the hell out of her. There was no doubt in his mind that she could take care of herself. The grin died on his lips when a flutter of white caught his eye. A piece of paper was stuck beneath his windshield wiper. He examined the parking lot. Nothing seemed out of the ordinary. Kinley had spotted the paper, too.

"Jesus loves you or two bucks off of your next oil change?" Her tone was easy sarcasm, but he didn't miss the way her right hand hovered around her hip—where she positioned her weapon.

"Let's take a look." He rounded his black SUV. Adrenaline pumped through his veins as he read the handwritten note clinging to the glass.

She was mine first.

He retrieved his cell phone and dialed his office. "This is Agent Adair. I need CSI down here." After relaying the address and enough of the situation for the time being, he looked at Kinley. She'd gone a few shades paler, her eyes wide as she stared at the script.

"Car." He shielded her with his frame. "CSI will see if they can pull anything from the scene. Maybe we'll get a fingerprint or two."

She nodded once and skirted around the back of her car to open the driver's side. Giving the area one last look, he got in the passenger seat and slammed the door shut.

"I'm being watched." Her voice was void of emotion. "For how long, I wonder?"

"He's getting bold. It's broad daylight. Anyone could've driven past. I need to get to a computer." The place he was most powerful was behind a monitor, hands on a keyboard. He could slip into the dark web, hack into any surveillance camera, and draw data from beneath every virtual stone. "We need to find a safe place for you, and I need to bring the FBI in on this."

"I'm not hiding. If I can draw him out just by living my life, I'll gladly try." Her hand was poised to shift into reverse, eyes locked on the rearview mirror. Imagine trying to live while the whereabouts of your worst nightmare were unknown. How she'd not only survived but thrived was beyond him.

"Right now, I seem to be the focus. That means he's not looking for another victim to snatch."

Sirens wailed in the distance, easing some of the tension pinching his shoulder blades. "Did you come here from your apartment or the police barracks?"

Her frown deepened. "Apartment."

"You said it yourself." Two cruisers took a sharp left into the parking lot. He gave one of the officers a chin lift. "He followed you. Knows where you live. Whether it's the Kingston Town Killer or some jackass looking to scare you, you're not safe. Your location is compromised. Is there someone you're close to? Friends, family in the area? Anyone you can hole up with for the time being?"

"And put someone else at risk?" Anger sparked in her eyes. "Not happening."

Dammit. She was going to be stubborn. Isolating herself wasn't going to help. He could reach out to Gus and Jules, two of his foster siblings, to see if she could crash there. A selfish part of him knew he could keep her safer. He glanced at her, such a fascinating combination of strength concealed by delicate features: the high porcelain cheeks, a petite upturned nose, lips set in a defiant scowl. Something surged to life inside him. Protective. Possessive. He was only feeling this way because she'd come to him for help. That was it.

Then, the solution hit him, settling comfortably into his gut. The only thing concerning about the idea was the instant sense of peace it gave him. He wasn't going to think too hard about his feelings. Not now. "Okay. You'll be safe enough with me."

"Whoa." She reared back, gaping at him. "Slow down. That's not what I meant. I appreciate the gesture, but I have a job to do. Cases that aren't just going to wait around while I hide in some safe room, leaving families to agonize over what happened to their loved ones. I have a place to go when I'm off the clock."

He'd pissed her off. Color saturated her cheeks, and her glare was intense and unwavering. "We'll swing by the barracks. Talk to the lieutenant and get whatever you need from your desk."

"I need to talk to your investigators. Give them more background than what you relayed to your colleague so they understand the situation." The guys from the FBI crime lab had arrived and were busy securing the scene.

"They can reach you at the barracks. The person you need to fill in now is your lieutenant." He was an asshole for being pushy, but she needed her network to know what was happening. Needed additional eyes on the situation. Kinley needed allies. "The lieutenant might be close to retirement, but he won't blow this off. He'll make sure there is an additional layer of protection for you. Trust your team to have your back. I know Gus will."

"I take care of myself. Have for a long time. I came to you first because this guy is probably using a self-destructing email account. With your reputation, if anyone could get additional information, it would be you. Please don't mistake my asking for help in this one area as a cry for help in others." She paused and took a shallow breath. "Do you want to talk to them?" She gestured toward the two local police officers. "Or should I drive?"

"Why don't you stay put while I talk to the local guys? I'll just be a minute." He hated leaving her in the car, exposed. He searched the tree line across the road, looking for anyone who might be lying in the wait. No one popped out, but that didn't mean whoever left the note wasn't watching somewhere nearby.

He got out of the car and walked over to the investigators. "You didn't waste any time getting here. Appreciate it."

A man and a woman who he recognized from the lab turned as he approached. "We got on the road right before rush hour." The woman surveyed the parking lot, eyes narrowed. "What's going on? Someone giving you trouble?"

"A friend of the family. This note might be connected to a prolific cold case. One that's going to need to be reopened. I want to know if there were any fingerprints left behind on this."

"If there are, we'll put it in the system and see if we can get a match."

He thanked them and took them up on their offer to take his vehicle back to the office before crossing to Kinley's car. He got in the passenger's side, slammed the door, and fastened his seatbelt. Silence hung between them until he picked up on the conversation they'd been having before he got out of the car to talk to CSI.

"We can go now. Tell me why you feel like you need to go it alone." The words came out harsher than he intended, but she didn't shrink from him. "You'd have no problem assisting someone else," he said more softly.

"It's different." Kinley reversed out of the

parking space, looking over her shoulder before trusting her back-up camera.

The tires crunched over the dirt and gravel coating the ground before lurching onto the smooth main road. "How?"

Her eyes darkened from honey to scotch. "They don't know what he's capable of. What would be in store if he took them or their children."

"Tell them. Make sure everyone knows exactly what will happen if he starts killing again—if he's even stopped. We can get him off the streets, lock him away for good, but we need to communicate with those who took an oath to protect." Her altruism was frustrating the hell out of him.

"It's not just that." She blew out a breath, ruffling a strand of hair close to her lips. "I was always curious about his profession. The investigators' profile was that of a middle-class male, white, most likely held a blue-collar job, and had higher than average intelligence. What if he's closer than we think? What if he always has been?"

"You think he's a cop?" Kinley was taking the exit toward Framingham. She was headed to the state police barracks.

She shrugged. "I don't know. Maybe. It would explain why he's evaded capture for so long. Staying one step ahead. Knowing the right way to dispose of the bodies so they can't be traced back to him."

"I can see it." They slowed to a stop at a red light. A school bus flanked them on the right and a small sedan on the left. "That's a good place to start. I'll pull the records for all public service workers in Kingston Town and those who repeatedly failed the police and fire academy. Too narcissistic to hack it as a team player. Someone who saw constructive criticism as a slight. We can see if there were any law enforcement transfers to Massachusetts around the time you moved. I want to have a look at the victims, too. If I recall, there were no specific traits shared, except for the age range."

"Some were runaways, and others were just in the wrong place at the wrong time. An opportunity too good for him to pass up."

Like her. She didn't need to elaborate. After Gus had told him about Kinley, he'd done some research of his own. Middle class, two-parent home, an only child. She'd gotten average grades in school and hadn't been in any real trouble. She would perceive his research as an invasion of privacy. She wouldn't care that the better he knew her, the more he could help to keep her safe. And he was doing exactly what she'd asked him not to— trying to take over, playing the role of protector. Was it out of gratitude because she'd saved his foster brother, or was he looking at her as someone who'd been abused? Someone like him and his biological brother. An innocent in need of protection.

"Tell me about your decision to move to Massachusetts." The light turned green, and traffic flowed forward. "I mean, medical care and education are huge draws, but as someone right out of college, it couldn't have been easy moving up here. Housing costs are through the roof. The cost of living itself is high. Especially for a new trooper." If she was surprised by his question, she hid it well.

"It didn't have to be Mass. I wanted New England, though. Somewhere drastically different from where I grew up. Where I could stop jumping at every shadow. Looks like they followed me anyway," she said casually and flipped on her directional. Easton spotted Gus's car in the lot of the brick building that housed one of the state police barracks.

"Did your family consider the move?" After almost losing their daughter, it would've made sense for the Wrights to want to be close to Kinley. Then again, he didn't have the best examples of paternal love.

"I never asked. They went through their own kind of hell when I was abducted. Polygraphs, interrogations, the media camped outside the front door. I know they love me. There are no hard feelings. We just needed different things. They found comfort in the familiarity of their community. I found it suffocating." The car jolted over a speed bump.

He nodded slowly, considering. "It must've been lonely."

"Loneliness won't kill you." She whipped into a spot and turned off the engine. "Thanks for looking into this, Easton. Gus said if anyone can find this guy, it's you. He'll give you a ride back to your office."

He raised a brow at her quick dismissal. Maybe she refused to hide out. He could understand and respect it, but that didn't mean he would leave her on her own. "Let me go in there with you to talk to the lieutenant. Together, we can figure out a plan to make sure this guy doesn't ambush you while you're doing your job."

The stubborn tilt of her chin told him his idea wasn't a popular one. "I get that you want to help. It feels good to have someone frustrated on my behalf, but this is a conversation I need to have with him alone. If I walk into my superior's office hiding in your shadow, how can he possibly trust my competence as a detective? I have cases that need my focus, and I'm not waiting around for a bodyguard or asking someone else to do my dirty work so I can hide behind a stack of papers." She shot him a fixed stare, begging him to object further.

"What are you afraid of?" Maybe she didn't want to be perceived as weak. Perhaps it was more than that.

Maybe she needed to be a crusader for victims, just as he did. If he was denied the ability to do his job, it would be a huge blow. If she helped enough people find closure to their own horrific tragedies, she didn't have to think of hers.

"How about my dignity and self-respect, for starters?" Her incredulous gaze stirred something within him. "Isn't that enough?" She unbuckled her seatbelt, the latch clicking as she shrugged it aside.

He was afraid for her. There was a tightness in his chest, which was stupid. She'd carried out her detective duties without issue this far. She didn't need someone to keep her safe. She needed an ally. "They're not going to think less of you. You won't be fired."

"I was out long enough dealing with the department's psych eval for the use of deadly force. I have to keep busy." Kinley turned toward the backseat, reaching beyond the center console to retrieve her bag.

The movement brought her body closer to his. Her scent hit him hard—coconut and sea salt—like she'd spent the morning on some sandy island beach. He drew in another breath. She was punchy and strong, but smelled like a piña colada and looked twice as sweet. The contrast between her outward appearance and inner strength was damn appealing.

"If I get put on paid leave, or taken off my cases..." She turned around, stopping midsentence. "I hate leaving things unfinished. He took away part of my childhood. I'm not going to let him rob me of anything else."

And, hell. What was he supposed to say to that?

Chapter Three

The day was so busy, Kinley didn't have time to think about the danger she might be in or the next steps she should be taking. She sure as hell thought about Easton, though. Getting the intensity of his gazes, the free-fall tumble in her belly at the most innocent touch, and the steady timbre of his voice to leave her mind was an impossible feat. She'd never felt the type of instant attraction she did with Easton. Her physical reaction to him was startling, but she wasn't afraid. Without a doubt, Easton was a good man. One who had painful secrets shuttered behind his dark eyes. He understood her in a way she wished no one ever had to. She still received counseling and took medication for her anxiety. It didn't shame her. Why should it? The steps she took to heal were as necessary as cleaning and covering a wound, setting a broken bone. But the majority of society shied away from discussing what it took to heal a soul. To the marrow of her bones, she knew Easton would never judge her. Would never question her personal journey.

The first thing she'd done was go straight to her lieutenant's office. She'd spent forty-five minutes convincing him that she was still able to do her job. Watching his face go from surprise, to shock, then pity wasn't how she wanted to begin the day. Maybe she should be grateful for all her years of anonymity. Now that she'd had a taste of being a normal person, not just "the survivor," it was hard to be treated otherwise.

"You look like you could use some sugar." Their dispatcher, Meredith Calder, rolled her chair to the other side of the sizeable v-shaped desk and pulled out a drawer. "Kisses or gummy peaches?" There was a reason they called the young woman Merry. She was the most considerate, kindest person in the station. Her drawer was always stacked with treats for her coworkers. That was just a stand-in for when she didn't bake. Her smile was like a thousand-lumen floodlight. Since she joined the barracks two years earlier, everyone liked to complain about needing new clothing stipends because they'd all gone up a size. Ultimately, Merry was the best-loved person in the barracks.

"Gummies. Thanks, Merry." She sank her teeth into the sugar-coated candy and leaned against the wall. Why did artificial fruit slices have to taste so good?

"Anytime, lovebug."

There was that, too. Her ridiculous nicknames. Ones that only she would get away with calling the intensely alpha personalities in the station.

The doorbell to the barracks chimed, and Merry glanced at the camera positioned on the front door before hitting the buzzer to allow the person access. Kinley instantly recognized the man. Merry's dad was friendly with the lieutenant and had been a decorated agent with the bureau before his retirement. Added to that, he clearly adored his daughter and was always bringing her coffee or lunch from the outside world. She might've learned to spoil those around her from her dad, but her physical features were all inherited from her late mother, who was originally from Mumbai. Merry had explained her mom was in a terrible car accident shortly after Merry's birth.

"There's my favorite daughter." Mr. Calder smiled at his child with such affection it gave Kinley a pang of envy. Her parents hadn't gone out of their way to keep in touch with her after she relocated. Then again, neither did she. Everyone coped with grief in their own way, but it still stung. "Thought you could use this." He slid a tall coffee through the glass window. "You stay up too late studying." Merry was just one more year away from earning her Master's degree to become a criminologist.

She rolled her eyes and giggled. "I'm pretty sure that's what everyone has to do in college, Dad. Thank you, though. I'll never turn down a caramel latte."

The sound of an incoming call made Merry straighten, her thick black hair swinging around her midsection as she reached for the phone, bronze cheeks falling with concern as she spoke.

She relayed the information of an unattended death over the radio to inform their shift, and Kinley straightened. "I'm glad I didn't go home yet. I'll respond." Working would keep her mind off Easton and her tormentor. Plus, she suddenly felt like she was invading a family moment—or maybe it was just her sense of isolation that made it seem that way.

"Be safe." Concern was evident in Merry's tawny eyes.

"Just another day at the office." She smiled and walked out of the dispatch room to her unmarked car. Talking to Easton had been a good thing. Her step was lighter as she approached the vehicle. Maybe she'd been intimidated, feeling a little cornered when he said he'd protect her in his home. Independence was important to her. Never did she want to be at the mercy of another again. Yes, Easton was a good man—she knew not everyone was a killer waiting to strike—but she needed to stand on her own. She didn't like to admit it, even to herself, but it was a great way to keep people at arm's length. She lived for her job. Lived to put criminals behind bars. To uncover deadly secrets. Now that she'd had some space, though, she realized it was probably something he'd just said in the heat of the moment. It wasn't like he was expecting her to throw together an overnight bag or something.

Kinley slipped behind the wheel, and the radio at her hip crackled.

"Badge thirty-four. Received. Responding to 18 Highland Path."

The voice was unmistakable. With everything going on, she was thrilled Lambert was responding to the same call as her.

Dusk was falling earlier each night. Colorful leaves peppered the trees and accumulated into dried-out piles on the sidewalks. Every few houses, a ghost, witch, or gravestone marked the coming of Halloween. As she reached the city's outskirts, the homes thinned, and the roads became more shadowed and coiled. There was a prickling sensation along her scalp as she glanced in the rearview mirror. No one was behind her. Nothing was wrong. She was just jittery from lack of sleep the night before and that email, plus the note left on Easton's car. Maybe that wasn't about her, either. Perhaps he had a girlfriend or lover, and someone was unhappy with their union. Something odd and ugly twisted her gut, but she dismissed it. What did she care if Easton was attached? He was only helping her. She had no claim on him.

She eased on the brakes as she approached the two-story home on a dead-end street. Silent blue strobe lights and yellow tape framed the property line. There was already a media van on site, Lord help them, along with an ambulance, even though it wouldn't be of much use. She parked behind one of the local cruisers and got out of her car. Strobe lights cut through the dark and illuminated boarded-up windows and a lawn overrun with coiled twigs and tall brush. Dead leaves clinging to the tall oaks lining the street rustled overhead. A car door slammed behind her, and she jerked around.

"I think that's the first time I've ever caught you

by surprise." Lambert had arrived, parked behind her, and exited his vehicle without her even noticing. How was that even possible? She was more preoccupied than she thought. In a job like hers, distractions were deadly.

"Don't get used to it. You made me realize I'm off my game, though. I appreciate the forewarning." She turned back to the house, and Lambert approached, standing at her side.

"This looks like every haunted house ever depicted," he muttered, hands on his hips, looking over the house from its boarded-up windows to the unruly landscaping.

They began walking toward a dilapidated Victorian. "It is giving off an Addams Family vibe." With every step closer to the old house, a sense of dread hollowed a pit in her stomach.

A gust of wind whipped her hair, so powerful it nearly made her lose her footing on the cracked concrete walkway leading to the front door. She continued with purposeful strides, keeping her hands at her side even though she was desperate to bring them together. She'd visited hundreds of crime scenes over the years and understood what to expect, so why did she feel so off-kilter?

"You okay?" Lambert's eyes narrowed as he glanced down at her.

"Yeah. Fine." She picked up her pace, brushing off his concern. The police officer guarding the door stepped to the side as they approached.

"What do we have?" she asked, stepping upon the threshold. He offered her a pen, turning the binder to note their information in the crime scene entry log.

"In my twenty years, I've never seen anything like this." The unmistakable scent of death wafted into the foyer. "Down the hall. The body's in the kitchen," the officer said.

She exchanged a look with Lambert before walking in the direction of the noise. The shuttering lens of a camera. The rise and fall of serious discussions. Everything seemed to slow as they approached the scene, like sprinting through waist-deep water. The crime scene photographer was taking pictures of the body at the kitchen table. She might've mistaken the woman for someone reading the newspaper if not for the rope holding the victim to the chair. Kinley absently dragged her damp hands down her pant legs.

"Detectives." A patrol sergeant approached them. "Scene's secured. This house hasn't had an occupant in over five years."

"Good. Fill us in." Lambert's eyes were trained on the scene around them, assessing, cataloging.

"Dispatch received an anonymous call to report an unattended death at three thirty. The caller immediately disconnected. Officer William Gardner was the first responding officer and gained entry through the front door, which was left open, at three forty." He lifted his chin toward the foyer where they'd been moments before. "Medical examiner declared the victim deceased upon arrival shortly after. We have officers searching the property and the yards of adjacent residents. The houses are spaced out in this area, but we're trying to locate a witness."

Kinley cleared her throat and directed her gaze at the patrol sergeant. "Any changes made to the scene that we should know about?" Even the smallest discrepancy at the crime scene could mean the difference between putting a killer behind bars or freeing them to walk the streets.

The sergeant rocked back on his heels, shaking his head. "Just an alternative light source. Wiring's faulty."

Kinley verbalized her thanks. The conversations blurred around her as she moved forward, flashlight gripped in the hollow of her hand. The deceased was dressed in black dress pants and a sensible blouse. Nondescript. Similar to what she wore daily. Her blonde hair had been hacked short—definitely not the work of a professional salon.

"No visible blood beneath the fingernails," she said as Lambert approached behind her, keeping his distance so they could both examine the body one at a time. "But maybe the ridges in her blouse caught some fibers. There's a newspaper beneath the left arm, but I can't tell if there's any significance to it. Once we release the body to the medical examiner, we can get a better look." She was babbling to retain some of the details she wanted to reexamine. It helped her remember the scene, along with the rough sketch she'd scratch into her notebook before the night was over. A swatch of yellow spandex material caught her eye, and she crossed the room, careful to place her feet where everyone else had also been walking to disturb as little evidence as possible.

"Lambert." She beckoned him over, and they started down at the floor. "What do you make of the cocktail dress?" It was tossed carelessly on the wooden planks as if someone had hastily stripped. Strappy platform heels were kicked off a foot from the piece of clothing.

"Maybe she was living here. Hiding from a domestic situation. Just got back from a club or a date." He looked from the body back to the dress. "Wouldn't you change into something comfortable, though? The clothing the victim is wearing looks like she's about to report to an office job."

"Yeah, and how often do you strip down to your skivvies in the middle of your kitchen?" she asked. The worn floorboards creaked as she shifted.

Gus raised a brow and smirked. "Now that Sasha's moved in—"

She put up both hands, stopping his next words. "Point taken. What if she was an escort or sex worker? Used this place as her home base? The price is right. It's secluded."

"So she entertains a john and then dresses for her other night job?" A door opened and closed somewhere in the house, boots scuffed down the hall, and radios crackled in the distance.

"It's possible. Let's see if we can get an ID on her. Must have a license or credit card somewhere. Especially if she's been living here."

Together, they methodically processed the scene of the crime. There was no sign of a struggle, no evidence of someone living in the vacant house.

"Where's the physical evidence? It's eerie." A shiver coursed down Kinley's spine. She just couldn't shake the idea that she was missing something big.

"No blood, no footprints aside from those believed to be the victims. The only tool marks we have are at the point of entry. If it weren't for the dress, I'd buy that she was killed elsewhere and dumped here," Lambert responded from behind her.

The strobes of their flashlights bobbed, and dust stirred as they moved down the stairwell in single file. By the time they'd reached the bottom, she was desperate to rub the gritty itch from her eyes. She refrained, keeping her hands at her sides. They were nearly back to where they started, with one wing left to process.

"First door on the right," she said, striding toward a room left slightly ajar.

They turned into the bathroom, illuminating the space. Long blonde hair, still in a ponytail holder, lay in the empty sink. Scissors sat on the vanity. She leaned away, revulsion pumping through her.

"You okay?" Lambert stepped forward. His features were shadowed, but the concern on his face was still readable.

"Fine." She gave a decisive nod, not sure if she was trying to convince her partner or herself.

"Tell me." Lambert's voice hardened. She only spoke of her experiences to a select few. He'd become one of those people.

She rolled her eyes, and steeling her nerves, leaned in to examine the hair more thoroughly. "Has anyone ever told you that you and your brother are both incredibly bossy?"

"Easton?" His brows scrunched up. "Easton's the smart one. The softie."

She nearly laughed out loud. Oh no, she'd seen Easton with her own eyes. There was nothing soft about the man. Maybe he wasn't as much of an alpha as Lambert or Isaac, his biological brother who was a SEAL operating overseas on a covert mission, but he was all man.

"Is that so?" She raised a brow. Easton certainly hadn't seemed like a pushover to her. "When the Kingston Town Killer took me, he cut my hair. He wanted me to look a certain way. Seeing that just dredged up some bad moments."

"Do you think that's what happened here? It would explain the positioning of her hand around the mug, why the body was sitting in a chair." Lambert's brows drew together.

"And the clothes." A breathy whisper shuddered from her lips. "Goddammit. The clothes." Ice trickled through her chest, coating her stomach with a cold, hard layer of fear.

"What? Lambert took a step closer, crowding her in the small bathroom. What is it?"

"I didn't think of it before. When I saw the clothing, I thought it looked like something I might pull out of my closet. It's business casual. Millions of people probably wear the same thing each day. But the hair, short like mine. The coloring and build of the victim." She dropped her gaze and swallowed hard. She had to be wrong. If she wasn't, an innocent woman had been killed because they shared a likeness.

"We need to get a look at that newspaper." A muscle in Lambert's jaw clenched.

She was breathing way too fast as they made their way back to the deceased. Despite the chill in the air, a bead of sweat dripped down her back. There was a chance this had nothing to do with her. Since her abduction, her mind went dark places, and the worst-case scenario was usually the first to pop into her head. Her heart was darting against her ribs by the time they passed through the threshold of the kitchen. The medical examiner was there, and the body was laid out on a white sheet.

"Where's the newspaper that was on the table?" Her voice was tight, stress squeezing each syllable.

"Bagged for evidence."

"We need to take a look at that. Nothing's supposed to be moved until the scene is released."

The investigator shrank back at the bite in Lambert's words, turned, and retrieved a clear evidence bag, placing it in his waiting hands.

She was barely aware of Lambert's fingers wrapped around her arm. There was a roar in her ears so loud she couldn't hear a word Lambert was saying. Sure, his mouth was moving, but there was no sound. The article twisted her focus up in a familiar web of the past. A picture of her—braces, freckles, cheeks pink with a summer sunburn—was visible through the evidence bag. *Community Fearful After Teen Abduction.*

"He staged the victim to look like me."

Chapter Four

Easton slammed on the brakes, jerking forward as his pickup truck came to a stop on Highland Path. The text he'd received from Gus had provoked something feral inside him. The abuse Kinley experienced as a child left him sick to his soul, but now to come after the woman she'd become? Abhorrent. That someone had taken another life as some kind of ill tribute to Kinley, dressing the deceased to play the role, left a metallic taste on his tongue. If he got his hands on the person responsible, he'd revel in making them regret ever laying eyes on Kinley, on any child. He closed his eyes briefly, numbing himself to the memories assaulting him. Decades later, he could still feel their hands, some rough and calloused, others smooth and cold, grabbing for him. He tried not to dwell on his childhood, but some things brought old terrors simmering to the surface.

He killed the engine and stepped down from his vehicle. A reporter was recording a clip beneath the sheen of spotlights directly in front of the house. He'd shield Kinley as best he could from the media, if needed. Oh, they wouldn't know who she was, or details of the victim found within the house, but they might badger her for an interview. Gus would finish processing the scene, and he had already spoken with their lieutenant regarding the connection between Kinley and the homicide.

Cold metal met his palm as he slammed the truck door and walked in long, purposeful strides toward the house. The reporter held out their microphone, asking a question as he passed. He simply ignored their presence. His priority was seeing to Kinley's safety.

"Stop there." The officer at the door stared down at him, suspicion clouding his expression. A cold gust of wind raked his hair. "Only authorized personnel beyond this point."

"Agent Easton Adair. FBI." He showed his credentials, and the officer's posture instantly eased a fraction. "I'm here to escort Officer Wright from the scene." He wasn't on official business, but he'd filled in his immediate director about the possible emergence of the Kingston Town Killer. As a member of an elite cyber squad, he often worked internally within various agency departments. If the FBI formed a task force to investigate, he wanted to be part of it. More than that, though, was the driving urgency to get Kinley somewhere safe. His physical and emotional reaction to her was baffling. He recognized himself in her—a human broken with thorough and agonizing force. Someone brought so low and desperate, it was a miracle they were able to claw their way out of the depths they'd been dragged. After he helped her, he'd go back to his one resounding mission. Stopping trauma before it happened.

Kinley appeared just beyond the threshold. Her features were set, any sign of emotion locked down tight. Her chin was high as she took the first step toward him. A satisfied breath filled his lungs, and he walked up the stairs, erasing the distance between them. Kinley's insides must be quivering, but the façade she projected was one of calm composure. She impressed the heck out of him.

"I told Gus I could get out of here on my own. I'm sorry he called. Besides, I drove here."

"Two troopers have already left to pick your car up. They'll bring it to the barracks."

More reporters had gathered outside, and a camera flashed from the crowd. A low growl reverberated in his throat. He had to make a conscious effort not to tuck Kinley into his side and rush her to the truck. She'd hate that. Rebuilding her self-identity must've been an uphill battle, but she'd done it. She was law enforcement just like he was, and she could more than hold her own against any threat. Still, he had her back and walked on the side closer to the reporters so she didn't have to. Their shouted questions rolled off his back as they strode quickly to the truck. Visibility was low, with the only light source from the news station equipment.

"Kinley Miller," someone shouted. The probing call didn't break their stride, but they both stiffened. Someone had uncovered Kinley's identity, and reporters were circling hungrily, scenting a breaking news report in the making. "Is it true you are the lone survivor of the Kingston Town Killer?"

"Is this investigation linked to the serial killer?" a male reporter called out. They started closing in on them, shuffling through the dead leaves and clutching their microphones.

"Has he contacted you?"

His hand hovered over the small of Kinley's back, and he moved closer to her.

"Was a child being held inside the house?"

Voices were more high-pitched and desperate as they continued to walk, and one man stepped right into their path. Adrenaline shot through him.

"Back up." The fury in his voice was barely restrained, and his calm shattered when the man didn't budge. "Get the fuck back." Without waiting, he put an arm around Kinley, just as he swore he wouldn't, and shoved past the reporter.

When they reached his truck, he opened the driver's side and rushed her inside. The moment the door slammed behind them, he threw the vehicle in reverse to put some distance between them and the media.

"What the hell was that?" Her voice shook, color high on her cheeks. "How did they find out my identity, and why did you shelter me? The suspect could've been watching in the crowd." She pinched the bridge of her nose. "Now he's going see me being coddled, assume I'm weak."

"It took him over a decade to find you. That makes you the opposite of weak. I no sooner would've left you to that pack of wolves than you would've hesitated to pull the trigger when a weapon was trained on Gus and Sasha." He took advantage of a wider section of road, cutting the wheel and shifting the truck into drive.

"That was different." Her voice had lost some of its heat. He got it. Really, he did. It was why he hadn't touched her when they left the crime scene—only reaching for her when a clear threat presented itself. He'd do it again.

The truck bumped down the unpaved street, jerking over divots in the road. "No. We're trained to protect. It's who we are." He stole a look, but her eyes were already locked on his face. He found himself tangled up in a gaze that packed one hell of a punch. Lust quivered low in his gut, coiling in the junction of his hips. Tearing his eyes away, he focused on the road in front of them.

She sighed, head lolling back against the seat. "Until I'm in mortal danger, trust me to do what I've trained for my entire life. Interfering any earlier tells me you think less of my skills. A partnership between Gus and me works because he sees me as an officer, not a woman who needs to be protected."

"Shit, Kinley. I don't think you're incompetent. I saw a threat and wanted to get you the hell out." He glanced in his rearview mirror. There was no one behind them on the lightless road. "I'm very aware you're a woman, but not in the way you think. I'd feel just as comfortable having you show up to an emergency call as I would any man—probably more because you've walked to the other side of hell. You rattle me. Bring something out in me that might be best kept locked away." He'd said way too much and not enough. Talkative, he was not. Around her, though, he wanted to spill all his secrets. Chat about her favorite food, find out if she read or binged Netflix shows in her free time. These urges weren't his norm, but he couldn't bring himself to care. Not if being more open would bring him closer to the woman beside him.

Her gaze was on him. She was sizing him up just as surely as if she'd reached her hand out and grabbed his arm. "I don't know what to say to that." Her voice dropped, and if it were even a fraction lower, her words would've been lost in the hum of the heater.

"Nothing is probably best, then." That was the truth. Keeping her safe came first, before his desire to get closer. "There's a higher-up at Seven News who owes me a favor. Let's see how his reporters figured out your identity." He used the vehicle's voice dial to initiate the call.

The direct office line rang once before a man picked up the receiver. "Justin Mancuso."

Must be busy for the man to be working at nearly nine o'clock. "Late night for you. Do you live at the station these days?"

"Agent Adair. How the heck are you?" The station exec's smile was audible through the line.

"Depends. You're on speaker. I'm currently driving away from the scene of a homicide." He turned on his directional and took the exit for downtown Framingham, toward Kinley's apartment. "Running, actually, from your evening news reporter. I have Kinley Miller in the passenger seat."

There was a beat of silence. "No, shit." The man mused before catching himself. "Sorry, Ms. Miller. You've been the hot conversation for the past few hours. Everyone and their mother is talking about you."

His jaw tightened. "We want to know how. She's lived in Mass for years. Never been bothered. Who gave her up?" Someone was fucking with her, and he didn't like it. Not one bit.

"We received an anonymous email to the tip inbox—and from what I've heard, so did every other news station in the area. Pictures, address, social media accounts. It was written as though Ms. Miller were sending it herself. Said she was ready to tell her story. I'll track it down and fax it to your office." The severe clip of Justin's voice pleased him. The man would send him the information he needed. In the meantime, he'd keep Kinley close.

"Forward it to me, too. I need to see it right away." Instead of stopping at her apartment, he drove right past. She didn't protest. Her brow was creased, frustration evident on her face as she studied the two news vans parallel parked in front of her building.

"Of course. And I'm sorry to you both for any trouble you encountered tonight. I'll talk to the team."

"The local PD might need a statement," he said.

"I'll contact them in the morning. Take care."

When they ended their conversation, he glanced at Kinley. Her eyes were closed, body rigid.

"We can't go to your apartment. Not without giving whoever set this up the satisfaction of watching you fight through reporters to get into your building."

"I know. Drop me at the barracks. Won't be the first time I've spent the night at my desk."

"You need to eat. Rest. Have some time to decompress. I have three spare bedrooms in case my family ever needs to crash at my place. You have your pick. I have spare toothbrushes in the closet. They'll be big on you, but I have a shirt and sweats you can sleep in." The image of her in one of his shirts, the hem hitting her knees, made his nerve endings snap to life.

"I appreciate the offer, but I hardly know you. It would feel weird to be in someone else's space right now."

"So would sleeping upright at your desk. Listen, you don't have to say a word to me all night if you want to be alone. I get it. I'm not easily offended. If you want to chill on my living room couch and hog the television? That's fine. Raid my refrigerator and pantry? That's cool, too. I can make dinner and leave it at your door like a bed-and-breakfast if that's what you want. I don't care what you do in my space. I just want you close."

"Why?" Her golden eyes narrowed.

He spared a glance at the road, then turned his gaze to Kinley. "Because you're important to Gus, so you're important to me, and no one should have to face something like this alone. Because you're the definition of strength and overcoming adversity, and it's an honor to offer help in any way I can." Satisfaction filled his lungs when he saw something more than suspicion flicker over her face. Her jaw dropped, full lips turning into an *O*.

For the first time since he'd started driving, the cab of the truck was silent.

Chapter Five

Kinley sat on her hands to stop them from shaking. One moment she was living the life she wanted, and the next there was a dead woman, reporters camped out in front of her apartment, and presumably a killer taking care of unfinished business—her. That reporter had scared the shit out of her when he stepped in their path. She hadn't been angry at Easton for shielding her. She'd been mad at her reaction. Tucked into his side, she felt safe in a way she didn't know was possible at this point in her life. She'd seen and experienced things she couldn't unsee or unfeel—so had he—but despite that, they both committed their lives to protecting people. She shouldn't need someone to lean on. Others were supposed to look to her for help.

And had she tried to wriggle free and stand on her own two feet? Nope. If anything, she'd clung to him. So much for the independent, kickass detective. If there wasn't a picture of her in Easton's arms plastered on tomorrow's headlining news, it would be a miracle. She felt guilty for giving him a hard time when all he was trying to do was protect her. If their roles were reversed, she would've done the same thing to keep him from the press.

"What are you thinking so hard about over there?" The hoarse roll of his voice made her stomach tumble into a freefall.

"How much my life has changed in twenty-four hours." She sighed and turned to him. "And how I appreciate you shielding me back there, even if I've been a jerk about it." She hoped the sincerity came through in her voice. "Seriously, you took time out of your schedule this morning to hear my concerns, then for Gus when he called you to the scene, now you're letting me crash at your place…"

"Stop." He flipped on the directional and pulled onto a residential road. "None of those things are a hardship." At the end of the street, they reached a cul-de-sac, and Easton entered the driveway of a huge, two-story colonial home. Motion-sensor spotlights illuminated the house. "I don't want you to presume I have pure intentions, here. I'm not just helping you. I'm trying to crack a notorious cold case. I don't mind helping people out, but I'm no do-gooder. I can be a selfish bastard, and most of the time, I'd rather spend hours at my computer than talk to a human. I go out of my way to avoid interactions. If someone gets too friendly at the local sub shop, I'll never go back. When it comes to household chores, I'm lazy. I've never mowed the grass at this house once. I don't even own a lawn mower."

"Well, thank God you cleared that up. I was wondering how you could be single." She shrugged her shoulders. "I live off frozen, sodium-laden single-serve meals because I just can't be bothered. Sometimes, I'll skip showering in lieu of reading a good book. I sneak into my apartment some nights so my elderly neighbor doesn't talk my ear off, and I never leave candy for trick-or-treaters."

"You want to date me, Kins?" A ghost of a smile flitted around his lips. One that made the breath get trapped in her lungs.

She rolled her eyes, hellbent on restraining the grin eager to spread over her face. "That's what stuck with you, huh?" This was silly. She had bigger things to occupy her mind than how Easton would look naked. Still, the image she'd conjured up was quite tempting. Annoyed with the giddiness fizzing in her belly, she unbuckled and opened the door. Easton was rounding the vehicle before her shoes hit the pavement. The temperature had dropped another few degrees. Spindly branches thrashed at the whim of the gusty wind, exposed to the elements without the cloaks of leaves. Easton's strides were long and purposeful, but she kept the pace, walking hip to hip with him until they'd reached the side door. Instead of inserting a key into the lock, Easton took out his cell phone and entered a code. The deadbolt disengaged, and he stood to the side so she could enter first.

They stepped into a mudroom with a built-in wooden bench and coat hooks on the wall. Footwear was stacked on a shoe rack on the floor. She removed her jacket and slipped it on one of the hooks, then followed his lead and removed her shoes. The room led into an open kitchen and living room. Light stone counters popped against the deep mahogany color floors. She'd been expecting more of a bachelor pad, but the space was sophisticated and welcoming. The walls showcased canvas portraits of his siblings, and a cozy throw was draped over the buttery leather couch.

"Your home is beautiful." Her apartment was a place to sleep and keep her stuff. She shifted as she looked around, suddenly uncomfortable with the inadequacy of her own residence.

"It would be a barren shell if it weren't for Jules. She chose paint colors, décor, and all the finishes. I didn't understand what was wrong with white walls and a futon, but I can't complain about the end result. It's comfortable, but it looks nice too."

"More than nice. Your sister could make a living as a home decorator." She was suddenly aware of just how alone they were in the large house. The only sound was their breathing in the cavernous space.

Easton cleared his throat and rocked back on his heels. Had the same thought crossed his mind, too? "She wants to be a behavior analyst. Help kids with special needs. Come on. I'll show you the spare rooms." He lifted his chin toward the staircase. The smooth floor was slippery against her socks, so she proceeded with caution, perfectly content walking at a slower pace.

"She's a good person," she added as they moved to the second floor. "After Sasha was rescued, she and Jules insisted I go to their favorite day spa to celebrate."

His eyes widened before he neutralized his expression. "I had no idea. Jules has a big heart. She's definitely the best of us." Easton opened the first door on the right. "She usually stays in this room because there's an ensuite. It's probably the most comfortable, but you can decide."

"This is fine. Thanks." It was more than fine. A queen-sized bed with a mountain of lemon-colored pillows, some with ruffles, others with sequins or beading lined the upholstered headboard. There was a large, cream-colored desk that matched the walls, and a pink crystal chandelier cast the room in a soft sheen. Before she'd been taken, she liked to paint her nails and chat about boys during slumber parties with friends. That girl had been left behind in the basement. After her escape, she did her best to blend instead of trying to stand out. She was out of place in this room with all its pretty frills and eye-catching details, but she might enjoy how luxurious it felt for a day or two.

"Okay," he said, tucking his hands into his pockets. "Let me get you clothes to wear. I'll make something quick to eat, and we can talk about what I've found so far. Sound good?"

A shaky breath escaped her lips. She hadn't expected him to find something so soon. The tightness in her throat made it difficult to speak, so she nodded and Easton disappeared down the hall. It took only a minute for him to return with a pair of sweatpants, a long-sleeved shirt, socks, and a hoodie. "In case you get cold," he said, handing over the stack of clothing. "I'll be downstairs when you're ready."

Kinley shut the door and shed her work attire. The stench from the scene clung to the fabric, and she was grateful for anything clean no matter how baggy it was. The pants were soft and lined with fleece. She pulled the strings at the waist taut so they wouldn't slip off. The hem of the shirt hit her knees, and the hoodie swallowed her up. She'd never been more comfortable. The fresh scent of Easton's laundry detergent hugged the material. Not that she'd ever admit to inhaling his things. Still, for whatever reason, being in his clothing, in his home, grounded her.

The scratch at the base of the door made her take pause. Easton hadn't mentioned having a dog. When she opened the door, the largest feline she'd ever seen mewed loudly and stalked past her. Its yellow fur puffed up at odd angles, and it seemed to be missing half of an ear. There were many sides to Easton she'd yet to uncover. She sought him out, padding down the hall and the stairs.

He was standing at the stove. His broad shoulders were lined with hard muscle, and they bunched as he transferred something from a frying pan to a plate. He turned, spatula in one hand and the plate in the other, and caught her eye. Her mouth went dry as he studied her. The expression on his face was primal and heated, and her heart banged against her ribs as she became adrift in his gaze.

"Looks good on you."

A current of electricity tingled through her at the

hoarse timbre of his voice. It reached the core of all the neglected, sensual places she'd ignored for so long. Places that were no longer silent. No, every inch of her flesh was smoldering.

"It's cozy. Thanks." When he gestured to the kitchen table, she pulled out a chair and sat. She wasn't sure her legs would hold her much longer anyway. One look from Easton and she'd gone weak in the knees. The plate clinked against the table as he set grilled cheese and soup in front of her.

"If there was ever a time for comfort food, now's probably it," he said before turning back to the counter.

"Thanks." The mouth-watering aromas of butter and melted cheese rose up to her nose, and her stomach grumbled in response.

Easton carried his own plate over to the table and sat across from her. She tried to ignore the way the muscles in his jaw clenched as he dug into the meal. Chewing had just become sexy as all get out. They ate in companionable silence for a few moments.

"So good," she murmured and swallowed down a bite. It tasted like childhood. "Knocks my frozen dinners out of the park." She wasn't exaggerating when she said most of her meals came from a square box.

"If that's all it takes to make you stay, I'll keep 'em coming." The grin he cast her way muddled all of her senses.

"Plump me up so I can't pass through the doorframes?" She laughed, unsure when she'd started sounding so carefree. Ironic given the circumstances.

"Whatever works." His smile widened, and he pushed back his plate. When she'd finished too, he cleared the dishes. "Want to talk here or in the living room?"

"That couch has been calling to me." The chair

scraped against wood as she stood up and made her way across the room. She sank down near the left arm of the furniture, sighing at how wonderful the cushions felt beneath her. "I could sleep here and be perfectly content."

"I'd feel better having you on the second floor. The alarm system will trip the moment someone walks onto my property, then I have a house alarm for backup. I don't think we were followed here, but we should be cautious." The cushion beside her dipped when he settled next to her. Not so close that she was uncomfortable, but not so far away she'd miss his masculine scent that beckoned her closer. Just having him beside her soothed the tension in her muscles. If someone broke into the house, she had no doubt Easton could protect her if it came down to it. She would protect him in return. Two sets of tactical training skills were better than one.

"I didn't see anyone, either." She tucked her legs beneath her, angling her body toward Easton. "Were you able to trace the email account?" With white knuckles clenched tight against the top of her thighs, she waited for him to deliver the news.

"The person who contacted you used a burner account, but fortunately for us, the sender's email didn't self-destruct until after twenty-four hours." He raked his hand through his hair, and the strands fell back into place. "These email sites offer more privacy protection than your average mail account, but they're only as effective as the user's knowledge. The sender failed to strip the metadata from the attached file, and they didn't bother to encrypt their connection. Maybe they didn't think it was necessary to send the email through an intermediary server. The sender either assumed the disposable email was enough to cover his trail or he wanted us to know his location." He studied her face, and her nerve endings twisted in response. He was going to tell her something she wasn't going to like. "The IP address belongs to a coffee shop in Grafton, about twenty minutes from here."

She couldn't breathe. Couldn't blink. Easton's words were a shock to her system. It was as though every part of her paused. The fear that had once immobilized her, fear she'd thought she'd overcome, flooded into her system, bursting through a dam of denial. Horrors of the past bombarded her senses. Easton was saying something to her, but she couldn't seem to hear. Then a hand came around her waist, another behind her legs. Strong hands lifted her. She was no longer sitting on the couch, but on Easton's lap. He held on to her tight, pulling her into the protection of his solid chest. Nothing could sweep her downstream when she was bound in his embrace. His touch didn't stop the panic attack but reminded her if she just held on and weathered through the crushing pain in her chest, she'd come out on the other side.

"That's it. Breathe, Kins."

How long they sat there, she wasn't sure. She just knew she wasn't ready for him to let go. His hands were still a vise around her as he murmured soft reassurances against the top of her hair. Heated breath ruffled the strands and tickled her scalp, sending goosebumps coursing down her arms. No one had ever witnessed one of her panic attacks. It had always been a fear of hers to experience such a private moment with another. Easton wasn't slowly backing out of the room though, or telling her to get a grip. He was just there, supporting her, holding her. His compassion made her eyes sting. She'd been on her own for so long that it felt good to be held.

"I—" she tried, but her throat was dry and clogged with fear. Without a word, he stood, cradling her in his arms, and walked up the stairs to the second floor.

With gentle hands, he placed her on the frilly yellow bed, pulling the comforter out from under her. He pulled the blanket up to her shoulders and tucked the material around her sides. When he straightened, new fear penetrated the depths of her soul. She didn't want to be alone with the shadows closing in, but she couldn't ask him to stay. Squeezing her eyes shut, clenching her teeth together, she waited for him to walk out of the room. Instead of the door shutting though, the mattress squeaked and dipped. She pried one eye open to find Easton lying on top of the comforter beside her. The weight of his arm flung over her side soothed her, and after a moment, she was able to speak the words she hadn't been able to earlier. "Part of me can't believe he's so close. The other part of me knows it's true because I have this awful dread building up inside me."

"You were a teenager when you escaped him the first time. Imagine what you can do now as an adult. An adult who is fully trained in law enforcement and has a career dedicated to hunting down killers. We're going to crush him, Kins, and you are not alone this time. You know he's here. We know he's here. By sunrise, the FBI, state police, and every local department in New England will know, too. This guy is going down." His voice held so much conviction, it bolstered her weakened resolve.

"I can't shake the feeling that he has a special kind of torture in store for me." A shiver quaked through her, and Easton tightened his grip. "The thought that he could harm others trying to get to me, like that poor woman tonight, makes me more afraid than I ever was before."

"There's nothing we can do right now, so sleep. I'll never let anything or anyone touch a hair on your head."

Her eyes filled again when he pressed a kiss to

her forehead. No one had ever stood up for her like this before. Guarded her while she slept. Lying with a man she didn't really know should feel awkward. Instead, a stillness settled over her, a sense of long-awaited peace. There would never be a worse time to get involved in a relationship, but she needed the comfort he was offering. She closed her heavy lids. She might regret it in the morning, but tonight, she was safe. Tonight, she'd fall asleep in Easton's embrace.

Chapter Six

Easton kept his eyes open long after Kinley's had closed. When her breathing finally deepened, he got out of bed to retrieve his laptop, then sat at the ivory desk so he could keep watch and notify the bureau of his findings. Right now, he was a physical barrier against whoever wanted to do her harm. Still, the sooner he informed all local law enforcement entities about the threat to a fellow officer, the sooner she'd get protection wherever she went, too. He'd gotten back into the bed and fallen asleep beside her, lulled by her soft snore, sometime after two o'clock in the morning.

The perpetrator was too close to Kinley. Her reaction last night was minor compared to what she must be going through on the inside. When the panic attack consumed her, he just did what felt right. Holding her in his arms and comforting her felt more than right. There was nothing sexual about his actions, but he couldn't help but notice how all her dips and curves tucked so neatly into him. There was never a time he'd experienced a connection like this, but he still had a job to do. Protect Kinley, get an evil serial killer off the streets, and come away with his heart intact. Outside of the love he had between his siblings, family had offered him little concern or protection growing up. Love had been a tool to manipulate and garner trust when the intentions were ruthless and damaging. Those closest to you could always inflict the deepest wounds.

Kinley stirred next to him, then her eyelids flew open and she sat upright in bed. It took her a moment to get her bearings, but recognition tempered the unease in her expression. She laid her hand over her heart. "I wasn't sure where I was." Her voice was breathless.

"You're safe," he said. Her hair was ruffled, and dark smudges had settled below her eyes, a reminder of what she was going through. Even still, she was the most beautiful woman he'd ever seen. It wasn't just her outward beauty that fascinated him, it was the integrity and courage that shone through her bright eyes. Her willingness to lay down her life for another, just like she had for Gus and Sasha. The selfless, generous nature Kinley possessed was the exact opposite of the selfish women, like his mother and aunt who cared for nothing but themselves.

"No one got near the property last night."

Kinley turned those gilded eyes on him, and it was his turn to be rendered breathless by what he discovered in their depths. Appreciation, trust, and above all else, a flicker of hunger that sucker-punched him right in the gut. He wasn't alone in his attraction. After the night she'd had and his own feelings so close to the surface, it was possible he saw what he wanted to believe.

"That was the first time I've slept without a nightmare in months." Her pulse bounded against the delicate skin at the base of her neck. "I'm just sorry I had to embarrass myself and blub all over you to get it."

"I'm not. I'd be worried if your reaction was anything less." He pushed a tuft of hair away from her face and tucked it behind her ear, withdrawing it quickly when he realized the intimacy behind the gesture. His fingertips tingled where he'd touched her as if the silky strands of her hair and the smooth curve of her cheek were still against his skin. Even though he'd held her through the night because of her distress, he couldn't deny wanting more moments with her in his arms. Kinley stared at him with wide, honest eyes as something sparked and snapped to life between them, filling the air with a surge of electricity. He stood, and the bed gently moaned with his receding weight. "I'm going to make coffee and breakfast. Take your time."

He started for the door, hating to leave her but needing a moment to regroup. On the outside, he might appear calm, but his insides were quivering with something he couldn't quite dissect at the moment.

"Easton."

He turned, and Kinley's eyes bored into him. He swallowed away the moisture that pooled in his mouth. She was so goddamn pretty.

"Thank you." The sincerity in her words almost made him pace back to the bed and hold her close like he'd done the night before.

There were so many things on the tip of his tongue. That it wasn't a chore to comfort her. That holding her had felt right. That he wanted to open up to her in a way he hadn't in a very long time. All the words jumbled together in his mouth, and he was unable to utter a single one. He gave a quick nod and left the room. A lame, inadequate response. If he opened his mouth, though, let all those thoughts tumble out, it would only distract from their real purpose. They had to act fast and get what leads they could from the café.

Once downstairs, he threw together a quick breakfast of cheese omelets and bacon. Slices of bread popped up from the toaster just as Kinley entered the kitchen. Her eyelids were still heavy, golden hair rumpled from sleep. Damn cute. She had changed into a pair of Jules's leggings and a long-sleeved shirt that he'd left out the night before. The fabric clung to her subtle curves. When he tore his eyes away from her body, she was staring at him with a look of interest that matched his own. Feverish blood roared through his veins. Her full lips were parted slightly, her eyes wide. He turned away and busied himself at the counter. "You take your coffee black, right?" he asked, just for something to say. He knew full well the answer to that question.

"Yes, thanks. It smells great. Anything I can help with?" She paused at the island, gaze roaming over his face. His chest clenched. He liked having her in his home way too much.

"No, relax. Everything's all set." He transferred the eggs to the two plates he'd set out earlier and turned off the burner on the stove. Kinley dragged out a chair at the kitchen table, and he laid a plate in front of her, along with coffee.

"I'm feeling a little spoiled." The shy grin she gave him made his stomach weightless.

"You've had a hell of a twenty-four hours. I'd say a little spoiling is in order." His fingers ached to touch the tips of her wet hair. Focusing on work had never been difficult for him. It was easy to get caught up in fettering out criminals from the dark web, setting up stings, and hunting leads and financial records. Now, though, he was caught up in Kinley, and that spelled trouble. He had to get his shit together because this could be the most important case of his career. The Kingston Town Killer was the definition of everything he worked his entire life to abolish. He brought his plate to the table and sat across from Kinley.

"I can't remember the last time I had homemade eggs and bacon. I need to start rethinking my lack of culinary skills." She had made a good dent in her plate, and his lungs filled with a rush of pleasure. What was it about caring for Kinley that made him feel on top of the world?

"I'd be happy to fill the role of instructor." He took a long sip of coffee, instantly more alert as the hot liquid slid down his throat.

Her smile lightened something heavy within him. "I'll keep that in mind. For now, though, I better focus on who is trying to send me a message." She took a deep breath in through her nose. "I'm ready to talk about the case. I just … last night was a shock. I hate that I wasted our time instead of putting one foot in front of the other."

"There was nothing we could've done last night. Now we can have a fresh start today with a clearer perspective." He lifted his fork and speared more eggs.

"So, we know that the sender used a disposable email to contact me, and they either didn't have the correct knowledge to cover their tracks fully, or they wanted me to know how close they were. If the IP address was traced to the café, that means everyone at the coffee shop was connected to the same network, right?" She picked up her last slice of toast and bit in with enthusiasm.

"Yes, but given the short-term nature of the account, we can place him there in the last twenty-four hours." As soon as he said the words, the breath rushed out of Kinley.

Her brow creased, and shadows clouded her eyes. Memories had taken her to a different time and place. Reaching his arm across the table, he took her hand and gave it a quick squeeze before letting go. Each time his skin touched hers, even when they sat close, talking, there was a bone-deep connection to Kinley he was unable to ignore. An inexplicable pull to know every detail about her life. Her favorite foods, music, and hobbies all seemed like pressing questions, which was kind of ironic given the gravity of their situation. Of all the other probing they needed to do to uncover information about the killer.

"Does the coffee shop have surveillance?" she said after a few seconds, pushing back her plate. Maybe she'd been full, or perhaps she'd lost her appetite with their discussion.

"No, but the adjacent gift shop has an outdoor camera that manages to catch patrons coming and going. The task force is getting a warrant as we speak." Last night, he'd hacked into the shop's video feed, downloading the file to his personal computer. The action wasn't legal, but he didn't want to risk the chance of the surveillance mysteriously disappearing. This person might have connections if they'd stayed off the grid this long.

"There's more to that statement. I can hear it in your voice. You've already looked at it, haven't you?" She perked up, leaning closer to him.

"You can read me better than most." He wasn't sure how he felt about that, only that it made the synergy between them seem more in synch. "I needed to look at the footage. With so many victims and so little information about the perpetrator, my gut's telling me he either is or knows someone in a position of power."

Kinley nodded slowly, and the ends of her hair fell in damp waves around her jawline. "I've always assumed he worked alone, but it's an interesting concept. Having someone on the inside to help him stay hidden would certainly be one way to evade being identified and captured. Or if he was in a position where he had access to information, he could stay one step ahead of law enforcement."

"That's what I'm thinking, too." He pushed his glasses up the bridge of his nose and focused on Kinley.

She lifted her arms, resting her elbows on the table. "I'd like to review the security feed, too."

He nodded, tilting his head slightly to the side. "I was hoping you'd say that. No one jumped out at me. You might recognize something or someone I didn't, though." They'd be far more productive if they worked together, and Kinley knew the Kingston Town Killer better than anyone, most likely. "I thought you might have an issue with me pulling the footage before the warrant. I know it's against protocol."

"I do like to clear the red tape before taking action, but the victims I get justice for are already deceased. We're hunting for a pedophile, a serial child killer whose psychological profile tells us he won't stop. I don't like those odds. I'd rather deal with any disciplinary action than have one victim on my conscience." A hard glint came into her eyes. Another box checked in Kinley's list of admirable qualities. She cared more about potential lives lost than getting written up for bending the rules.

The screen of Kinley's cell phone lit up a second before the trill of an incoming call. She reached for it, but not before he noticed his brother's name on the screen.

"Lambert, I'm going to put you on speaker," she said, taking her phone away from her ear and setting it on the table between them.

"Any trouble overnight?" There was a hint of stress in Gus's voice. Easton had messaged him last night to let him know of the overly aggressive reporters and the IP address of the first email.

"No. Did Easton tell you about the location where the first email was sent?" She lifted her eyes, gaze falling on him.

His brother hissed out a breath. "It's too close."

"Tell me about it." Kinley scrubbed her hands over her face. If there were anything he could do to ease the stress creasing her forehead, he'd do it in a heartbeat. "Is that the reason you're calling, though?"

"Not really." Gus sighed. "Got to work just now, and the parking area is gridlocked with media vans. I think you should consider working remotely today. Whoever contacted the news stations knew what they were doing. They wanted to disrupt your life. This is personal."

"And yet, would the Kingston Town Killer go to these lengths for revenge? If he knew your whereabouts, why not ambush you?" As soon as the words were out, Easton regretted them. She didn't need the mental image of someone hiding in a bush waiting to snatch her. "Last night's homicide victim was an adult. Our suspect's interests veer toward a much younger population. Why wouldn't he have gone back to his typical pattern and let Kinley find the body?"

The woman across from him didn't even flinch, and it wasn't because she was callous. She was determined and focused on the job at hand. The more time he spent with her, the more impressed he became. She was able to compartmentalize the fear and anxiety she must be experiencing.

"I've had the same thought, too," Kinley murmured. Her chair slid against the floor as she stood and placed her hands on her hips.

"You have been the arresting officer in many homicide cases. Some have gone to court in the last month alone. We shouldn't rule out retaliation." Filing cabinets sliding open, fingers tapping on keyboards, and the static of radios buzzed over the line.

"Or a stalker. Do you have anyone who would want to hurt you? Any past relationships that didn't end well?" He didn't want to ask about men she'd been with. The burning sensation curling in his chest made him take pause. He wasn't a jealous person, and it wasn't like he was in a relationship with Kinley. No matter how appealing she was, he had to remember she'd come to him for help. He wasn't going to let her down. Wasn't going to let the bureau down by getting sidetracked with thoughts about how good it felt to hold her in his arms. When Kinley shook her head, though, relief doused the agitated stir within him.

"There's something else." The wariness in his brother's voice made him tense. He stood and rounded the table to stand beside her. "A partial print was found on the collar of the shirt. We're running that through the system now. The other prints on the shirt that came back more quickly. They're yours, Kinley."

At her sharp intake of breath, he put his hand on the small of her back. She stilled, body rigid beneath his fingers.

"I didn't touch the body," she said in a quiet voice. "Where were my prints located?"

"The left shoulder." Gus's tone dropped an octave. Someone must've entered the room—someone he didn't want overhearing their conversation. "I know you had nothing to do with this, but I wanted to warn you that the lieutenant will be calling. Despite trying to convince him otherwise, he wants you suspended with pay while things are being sorted out. You have to be careful."

"This is a nightmare," Kinley mumbled, numbness clinging to each syllable.

He clenched his teeth. She shouldn't have to go through this.

Unfortunately, he was afraid the nightmare was just getting started, and someone was taking great joy in putting Kinley through psychological torment. They needed to put a stop to it before the perpetrator got their hands on her.

Chapter Seven

The call from the lieutenant came shortly after Kinley hung up with Lambert. She was officially placed on administrative leave. The department wanted to investigate her involvement in recent events and protect her from potential harm while on the job now that all signs were pointing to someone specifically targeting her. Bitterness was a smoldering coal in her gut, one that she couldn't pace away in Easton's living room. The leave didn't feel like protection. She felt like a suspect. Of all the things that had happened to her, this somehow was the hardest to bear, the most unfair.

"You need to work off some of that anger." Easton sat in an armchair, eyeing her with an unreadable expression. He was adept at masking his emotions on a whim. Suddenly, she felt like an outsider. Would Easton still be willing to help her now that she'd been placed on leave? Maybe he'd shut her out of the investigation altogether.

"I don't think that's possible." She paused in front of the sliding glass doors. The sky was a blinding blue, illuminating the piles of colorful leaves padding the ground. How ironic that the day was so vibrant when her mood was so dark.

"Won't hurt either way. Follow me. I'll show you my favorite room in the house." In a fluid movement, Easton stood and walked toward a door off of the living room. He must've been certain she'd follow because he didn't glance back to see if she was on his heels. Of course, she was. What else could she do?

He was already heading down a flight of stairs when she caught up. The wood squeaked beneath their weight as they moved. Basements weren't her favorite place, in fact, she went out of her way to avoid them, but she kept her mind occupied staring at Easton's broad shoulders. At the muscles that rippled beneath the material of his shirt. There was no musty, damp smell here—something that still made the fine hairs on her nape raise and her stomach queasy. No shadowed corners or dirt floors. The space before her did elicit a different reaction though. Shock.

"You put Planet Fitness in your basement," she remarked, taking in the equipment stationed around the room. A treadmill, stationary bike, and an elliptical machine rested on gray-planked flooring facing a floor-to-ceiling mirror. There were free weights, a bench press, and two punching bags positioned over a mat.

"I was a scrawny kid. Easy prey. Isaac was always bigger, but not by much. We learned fast how important self-defense was to our survival." A dark storm brewed in his eyes, but he blinked it away. "You're welcome to use any of the equipment, but I thought throwing some punches might help."

Easton kept alluding to his story. Maybe that meant he was getting more comfortable with her and eventually would share with her as much as she had with him. She wasn't sure why, but there was a strong sense of comradery between them. She did her best not to form close relationships, not wanting to have to place her trust or faith in anyone. The day those police sirens wailed outside her captor's home and then faded into the distance was the moment she resolved to save herself. She didn't want to depend on anyone, but she wanted to know Easton's story. Actually, she wanted to know everything about him, and that was troubling. "I think so, too. Thanks." She blew out a long breath, temporarily easing the lump that had formed in her throat when the barracks notified her that she was on leave.

They crossed the room to the bags, and Easton removed a set of hand wraps from a shelf stocked with water bottles and towels. He turned, and she nearly collided against his solid chest. The air in the room thinned as she struggled to fill her lungs. His masculine scent tickled her nose, making her yearn to bury her nose in his shirt or the crook of his neck. Easton's pupils expanded as he searched her face until his eyes were an inky black. Warmth broke through the anger bunched inside her chest, and it seeped through her belly to settle between her hips.

"Let me." His voice was hoarse as he unraveled the wraps. The weight of his touch steadied her trembling hands, grounding her. Easton took care winding the fabric from her wrists to knuckles and back again. God, he was beautiful. She'd known it before, but being this close to him was intoxicating. Her heart was firing in rapid succession. The only thing that made her feel marginally better was the pulse pounding at the base of his throat. His focus broke from the wraps on her hands and traveled up her body, pausing when their eyes locked.

For a moment, nothing but the intensity blazing over his features mattered. If he was the flame, she was the tinder. The fire reflected in his eyes jumped to her, igniting an indescribable need. These feelings were too much. Too overpowering and honest. For someone who had known true life-or-death fear, it seemed silly to be frightened of whatever was happening within her, but she was terrified. Clearing her throat, she retreated toward one of the punching bags.

Easton turned on the sound system, increasing the volume until heavy classic rock pumped through the room. Standing with her legs staggered and shoulder-width apart, she began driving her fists into the bag with a series of jabs and hooks. The dull thud of her hands hitting the bag was a welcome sensation, as was the slight sting in her knuckles. Easton was positioned behind the other bag, but she wouldn't look at him. One glance would, without a doubt, crush her focus.

"What's bothering you the most?" Easton's low, deep voice rippled over her as she landed a right hook.

She gritted her teeth. "Having my life interfered with." She panted. "Being punished over and over for the actions of the person who hurt me."

Jab. Jab. Hook.

"Get it off your chest, Kins," he murmured through his movements. "What else are you pissed about?" The chain anchoring the heavy bag to the ceiling rattled as Easton delivered a series of kick combinations.

"I'm mad that I'm afraid." The winded whisper couldn't have come from her mouth. Wasn't she done being petrified of what was lurking around the corner? Or was she able to be more honest with Easton than she was to herself? "That I'm still under his thumb. Weeks, months of detective work being taken from me while I'm on leave. It's not fair." Acid churned in her gut, burning along her esophagus as she choked out the bitter words. "Then my prints show up out of nowhere at the crime scene." She stilled, chest heaving. A cold bead of sweat trickled down her back.

"You remembered something." Easton paced across the room and killed the amplified music with the touch of a button.

"Someone wouldn't have needed to plant my fingerprints at the crime scene if the clothes the victim was dressed in were already mine." A slab of ice plummeted to the depths of her belly. "I had thought someone was trying to frame me for something. Maybe they're just sending a message."

"Of how close they can get to you." Silence surrounded them, the only noise their quickened breaths. "That's assuming those actually were your clothes at the scene. Who might've had access to your things? A gym locker? Laundromat? Friends who visited recently?"

A metallic tang coated her tongue. Shit. She'd bit her bottom lip. "I keep a few outfits at the station. Sometimes I get to the barracks early to work out before my shift. It's just easier to keep some stuff there instead of hauling things back and forth."

"Do you remember what you have at the barracks now?" Easton began unwrapping his hands like he was getting ready to drive there himself.

"With everything going on, it's hard to remember what I did yesterday." She released a long breath, flipping through her mental calendar from the past week. "I picked up my clothes from the dry cleaner. Wednesday maybe? I'm not sure. I took two of those outfits to the barracks and tossed them in the closet for emergencies."

"And did you wear either?" he asked, tossing the wraps back on the shelf.

"No. I've been so busy with my cases, I haven't used the weight room in weeks." Pain wedged into the base of her throat. Getting to the locker room closet at the barracks required access. If her clothes really were taken, it was most likely done by someone she knew, maybe had worked side by side with for a very long time. Wouldn't she recognize him, though? His voice?

"We need to see if those clothes are at the barracks." Easton's voice was hard, and something cold passed over his eyes.

"What was that look? Because you think the killer is closer than we thought or because our perp could be someone we trust?" The same thought was weighing on her. Was the person responsible for stealing so much of her childhood working with her on a daily basis? And if so, why begin tormenting her now?

"We talked about our suspicions that this person is someone in law enforcement, or has a family member helping them stay one step ahead, whether they know it or not. This is just one more supporting argument. I know you're angry about being placed on leave. You have every right to be, and it sucks. But I can't deny that I feel much better having you here, especially now, than being targeted at work." He stood before her, skin coated in a light sheen of sweat, muscles corded beneath his shirt. Looking at Easton like this and experiencing this indescribable pull wasn't where her thoughts should be focused, but damn.

Not only that, but the protectiveness heating his features comforted something inside her. It felt good not to be so alone. She wasn't imagining the interest flashing in his dark eyes—that much she knew, but even he had told her it wasn't a hardship to help her because it would get him close to catching the notorious Kingston Town Killer. Imagine what that would do for his career with the bureau. Maybe she wasn't totally a means to an end for him, but they wouldn't be here together if there wasn't a monster on the loose. Getting involved with Easton would be a self-destructive decision. Not because she was attracted to him, but because she liked and respected him. Those extra feelings could get complicated.

She blew out a long breath, releasing all the negative thoughts with a rush of air. "Whatever happens, please don't shut me out of the case. I need to be involved. Have a small part in his capture if possible."

"I'm not going shut you out. If I thought I could protect you from more pain, I might shield you from new information, but I know that would just drive you crazy, make you more unsettled." He rocked back on his heels, shifted his weight. "There's something I need you to do for me, though."

She raised a brow. "Okay. What?"

"When it comes down to the wire, remember how many families are seeking justice. That justice looks different to everyone." His tone dropped an octave, but his eyes never wavered from hers.

"You're worried I'm going to kill him. Don't think I can resist the opportunity to right a wrong." She shook her head. "I won't lie and tell you the thought of ending the terror he's caused doesn't give me some pleasure." There'd been times she'd even considered taking a leave from her work to try to hunt him down, but she'd committed to protect rather than seek her own revenge. "I'd rather see him behind bars, though. Prison won't be easy on him, and death would be too quick."

Easton nodded and took the wraps she'd unraveled, placing them beside his on the shelf. "I wouldn't blame you. Wouldn't judge. Thank you though, for being sincere with me. And while we're being honest, there's something else I should tell you."

"What's that?" She tilted her head and took a step closer.

"I feel a pull toward you. An intense kind of connection. I don't know—it's hard to describe. And I'm tripping over my words. I shouldn't have brought it up, but you should know despite how I feel, you're safe with me. I'd never hurt you or try to coerce you into anything. I'm committed to solving your case, regardless of how I'm feeling right now."

His words rocked her sense of equilibrium, but she steeled herself. "You're not alone."

"I'm not?" His breathing visibly increased, his ribs retracting beneath his fitted shirt.

She shook her head. "It's taken all of my professional resolve not to stare at your ass in the mirror." She gestured toward the wall-length mirror behind him. One she had a perfect view of as they'd been boxing. His lips quirked into a smile and he let out a small chuff. A warm glow expanded in her chest. It was nice to elicit the deep roll of his laughter. "I'm physically attracted to you, but it's more than that."

"For me too." His eyes were nearly black now, and when his tongue darted out to lick his lips, a liquid pull settled at the junction of her hips. "It would be a terrible idea, wouldn't it?"

"Probably the worst." Even as she said the words, her feet drew her forward. Each step took her closer to Easton. The air was thick with tension, lungs starved for oxygen because she didn't dare breathe for fear the moment would dissolve into nothing. She was so done with doing her best to feel nothing. The problem was that with Easton, she felt it all, and that was very, very dangerous.

Chapter Eight

Easton was momentarily stunned by Kinley's omission. She was drawn to him and felt the same indescribable connection that he did. With every step she took toward him, the reasons why coming together on a physical level was a terrible idea fled from his mind. His stomach clenched and tumbled as her hands skimmed up his abs, worked their way over his chest. Just that slight bit of contact had him rock hard and trembling. There was no way to hide his attraction. Not with gym shorts on and her hips flush against his. He lowered his head at the same time as she came up on her tippy toes. Their lips feathered together, gentle at first, testing. Then her tongue licked the seam of his mouth, and lightning crackled through him, jolting straight to his groin.

Fuck, this woman lit him up like a power surge. Heat like this was bound to explode at some point. His movements were clumsier than usual as he fought the urge to grind his hips against her. Her fingers were buried in his hair, hands anchoring the tilt of his head so she could control the depth and intensity of the kiss. He was happy to indulge her. In fact, with just one taste of her pretty mouth, he was starting to wonder if there was anything Kinley could ask for that he wouldn't give. How could he stay objective and keep her safe when she was turning him inside out?

Every time his hands brushed just below her breasts, she moaned into his mouth. God, he wanted her. Wanted her with an intensity that scared the shit out of him. They were both broken in ways that never really healed. He recognized her trauma, had lived through his own version of hell. How many times did he have to remind himself he was here to help her, not fuck her?

Maybe that was part of the problem. The feeling that if they crossed a line, it would never be just mindless sex. Kinley touched him on an emotional level, and he couldn't go there. To move past the betrayal of someone close to him—his own goddamn mother—letting her strung-out boyfriends beat on and abuse him and his brother—he'd forced himself to go numb. He buried that shit deep. Locked it down so tightly that those feelings of shame and betrayal could never resurface. If this thing went any further with Kinley and his heart got involved, all those emotions would come bubbling outward. He'd already thought of his past way too much since offering to help the woman driving him to the point of insanity with her sexy sighs and clever tongue.

With gentle hands, he gripped her shoulders to steady her and stepped back. They were both breathing hard. Kinley's lips were rosy from kissing him, her expressive eyes wide with shock and lust. At least he wasn't alone.

"Goddamn, Kins." His breath was still ragged, and he couldn't prevent himself from cupping one side of her face. From skimming his thumb up her cheekbone. Fuck, did it feel good to have her lean into his touch. This was a woman who didn't trust easily. Who was hellbent on maintaining her independence. She was giving him a bit of both though, and he'd never been more humbled. "That was—"

"Dangerous." She sighed and straightened her head, then took a step back, leaving his hand suspended mid-air. He dropped it to his side. "I can't afford to get sidetracked. It might cost me my life. Your life."

She'd picked her words carefully—*mine* and *yours*. Two separate lives with different paths. Until he'd met Kinley, he'd been all right being alone. Hell, he'd thrived on it. So why did it burn through his insides that she didn't say it could cost them *their* lives? After this was over, she fully expected to go back to the way things were before she'd asked for his help. The problem was that things were starting to get complicated for him. He didn't know what to do about it, so he took a step back. Better to analyze and assess than jump right into the fire he'd never be able to crawl out of.

"I'm not going to let anything happen to you, and I trust you to have my back." And he did. No one would get the drop on either of them—unless they were too wrapped up in each other to sense impending danger. Another reason to keep things as professional as possible with the beautiful woman in front of him.

Kinley nodded but said nothing.

"I need a shower before we dive into the case. Jules has a ton of shampoos and lotions in the shower upstairs. Use whatever you'd like." He swiped a bead of sweat from his forehead then walked over to the mini fridge in the corner of the room. "Water?"

"Please."

He tossed a chilled bottle across the room, and Kinley caught it with one hand. "I feel strange taking her things."

"She'd be miffed if you didn't. Once Gus lets it spill that you'll be staying here for a bit, I'd be surprised if she didn't stop by with provisions, or at least to say hello." He wrenched the cap off the bottle and took a couple of big gulps.

"I'd like to get to my apartment today." She sipped her water, then continued. "Grab some clothes and a few of my things."

"We'll make it happen, even if I have to go in to get it."

Her toned shoulders visibly relaxed, as though she'd been preparing for an argument.

She cleared her throat and recapped her bottle. "You think the media vultures are still circling?"

"Can't rule it out. I don't want that bastard having the satisfaction of seeing you on the news." A burn spread through his chest, and his jaw tightened to the point of pain. There was nothing he wouldn't do to keep Kinley out of that monster's grasp. One of the many reasons he needed to be objective, even if it killed him.

Her lips settled into a frown. "Yeah, that's just the image I want to portray. His victim packing up a duffle bag and running to the protection of an FBI agent."

"You have nothing to prove to him. Nothing." He ground his teeth together. No one should go through what she had.

Her tongue inadvertently darted out and swept across her lips. She opened her mouth as if to say something, then closed it. He also loathed the word *victim*. They were both stronger than their tormentors.

"Right. I'm going upstairs. Any chance you want to conserve water?"

Her words chased the breath from his lungs, had him hardening with the flick of a switch. His gaze traveled down her luscious body. Her breasts would be heavy in his hands. Hard nipples strained beneath her shirt. Fuck, he wanted to know what kind of sounds she'd make when he sucked and licked those tight peaks. Wanted to slide deep inside her wet heat and swallow her moans as the shower spray pounded down on them. But he wouldn't be doing any of that. Not today. Not when his heart and her safety were entangled with this feverish heat. He'd never had to work to keep his emotions in check when it came to sex. Kinley was different. Dangerous.

"No." The single syllable was clipped, and her

expression shuttered. Damn, he hadn't meant to hurt her. How did he explain that he was starting to fall for her, even before he'd tasted her sweet lips? "I can't lose my focus. Not now, and that's exactly what will happen if I join you in the shower."

Her cheeks pinkened, and there was a sinking sensation in his gut. He got the feeling it cost her to ask, that she didn't make a habit of sleeping around. Not that he'd judge if she did. "I'll meet you downstairs after, and we'll figure out the next steps." Her tone was professional and direct, as though they'd just met. He was the one who'd turned her down, so why did it bother him so much that she was erecting walls?

What a prick he was to flat-out refuse her and not explain. She must think he ran hot and cold. One moment he was admitting his attraction and more, and the next he was telling her he didn't want to take things further. Still, Kinley had voiced her hesitations, too. After that explosive kiss, she'd told him she couldn't afford to get sidetracked. Maybe her invitation was made in a moment of weakness. Maybe she didn't want to be alone with her thoughts. He was okay with her using him as an escape. What he wasn't okay with was her shutting him out because he'd been tactless with his words. A long breath whooshed from his lips as he made his way to the stairs. A shower would help to clear his head. He'd make it right the moment they reconvened. He wasn't sure when Kinley's emotions, her happiness, had become as important as her safety and solving the case, but they had.

****

Kinley was already at the kitchen table that had become their headquarters. They'd shared meals, fears, and secrets at those often-empty chairs, and despite the fact that she'd been in his home less than twenty-four hours, he was going to picture her here when she went back to her life. He wanted that for her. To finally be free of the man who violated and tortured her. Imagining her walking through his front door, though, made his stomach harden. There was something about this woman that threw all his beliefs and ideas about the future to hell. He crossed the room and pulled out a chair, wood scraping together as it slid over the floor. He sat and directed his focus at the woman who had him tied up in knots. Her hair was still damp from her shower, and there was a fresh, pinkish hue to her cheeks, like she'd cranked the water to a scalding temperature before stepping beneath the spray.

"Kins, about earlier—" He leaned in, bracing his forearms on the table, willing her to look him in the eyes and see his sincerity.

Her back straightened, and she folded her arms against her chest. "Listen, I'm not some fragile waif who's going to be a sobbing mess because I didn't get my way, so let's just drop it."

"Fragile is the last fucking thing I think you are. You're a goddamn gladiator. You've gotten under my skin, Kins. So far I don't even know what to do about it. I've spent my whole life keeping people at bay, and it's all I can do not to draw you closer. The way I feel around you scares the hell out of me. That was what my no meant earlier. I just didn't have the words."

"I thought you were worried I might have a flashback of the rape. That's why I moved away from home and changed my name. People look at you differently when you … when—"

"I know," he said in a hoarse whisper.

Kinley's eyes widened. She waited a beat, then two, the silence growing thick in the space between them. "Tell me." Her soft demand made him take pause.

He'd learned details of her horrific captivity at the academy in Virginia, and more from the details she'd told him, and yet he'd shared nothing about his own trauma.

"I never knew my father, and neither did my mother—if I can even call her that. Men were coming and going all the time. She used whatever money she had on her next fix, until she had squandered everything and the only thing she had to offer up was some alone time with one of her sons." His voice was detached. It was much easier to talk about when he could isolate and lock down his emotions. "My mother said if one of us told, she'd kill the other. We finally worked up the courage to say something to a teacher. Wish I'd done it sooner, but I was so afraid of gathering the nerve only to have someone not believe me, or think I'd encouraged it in some way. Law enforcement removed us that day. Some of the foster homes we were placed in were bad, but nothing like the dirty apartment where we spent the first decade or so of our lives. I've gone to enough therapy sessions to know that what those drug dealers did to me, what they forced me to do to them, wasn't my fault. Still have trouble talking about it. Only my siblings know, and now you, too."

The empathy in her eyes gutted him. Tears had pooled in the golden depths, but she blinked them away before they could spill. Fierceness stole over her face, and she stood. The chair clattered back, hitting the center island. She rounded the table and held out her hand. When he slid his palm against hers, she gave him a light tug, and he stood up. Her arms came around his torso, grounding him against the unexpected onslaught of hatred and disgust for what had happened to him and his brother, to Kinley. For millions of innocents suffering at that very moment.

"Where is she now?" Kinley asked.

"Dead." She should've had to answer for her crimes, be put through detox which would've been its own version of hell, and locked in prison for the rest of her days, but her heart had stopped with a needle in her arm. It was more peaceful than she deserved, but she couldn't hurt anyone else either. "She overdosed before her trial."

Kinley nodded into his sweater. "We chose a life of service, of helping instead of causing harm. No one can take that away."

"Because of what we've been through, there are some who won't have to." There was a prickle behind his eyes, and he tightened his jaw to push the odd sensation away. He'd worked hard to be physically and mentally tough. To never again be taken advantage of. And yet the tiny powerhouse in his arms had him blinking back tears. He hated to be touched, especially for comfort. Yet, last night, he'd held her, and right now, she felt so damn good against him, like she was made to fit into the crook of his shoulder. He was fucked.

He allowed himself a few more moments of bliss. He stood in the kitchen with late-morning light streaming through the windows, holding Kinley against him. He drew her summer-island scent into his lungs and committed to memory the way the soft strands of her still damp hair felt against his cheek. Then he stepped back slowly. "I need to touch base with my superior, then, we'll go across town to your place."

"Thank you." The sincerity in her voice was a reminder that Kinley wasn't used to reaching out for help. Except for his brother, Gus, no one had her back in a long time. It made him want to be there to catch her when she fell, or in Kinley's case, cover her while she leaped headfirst into the fray.

"You don't have to thank me. We all have something to gain from nabbing this guy." The sooner Kinley was free of this sick degenerate, the sooner they could move on with their lives.

Chapter Nine

Kinley stood with her back against the stone countertop, gripping the cool granite edge behind her. Easton was pacing the living room, discussing their plans with his boss in a clipped tone. Something about the conversation was grating on his patience. She could no longer lie to herself. Every shred of her being was turned inside out and tangled up by her rapidly developing feelings for Easton. Still, she couldn't forget the biggest reason he was helping her. She was the means to capture one of the most notorious child predators of the century. Oh, she was intimately aware of how important it was to shield society from her abductor. Part of her had thirsted for vengeance since the moment she slid through the broken basement window of her prison, but she'd locked it down. Eventually, the drive to work in law enforcement had tempered her desire to seek revenge, though it was always there, part of her, like the blood that pulsed through her veins.

Easton abruptly turned, shoving his cell phone into his pocket. She was overwhelmed by his bravery to overcome such a horrific childhood. Her heart ached for him, but she was moved beyond words that he would trust her with the truth of his past. "Everything okay?" she asked.

His lips were pressed together into a thin white slash. "My superior wanted me to report in for an additional brief. She told me to head to the satellite office while you gathered your things at the apartment."

"Is that the new plan?" Her heartrate sped up, and she hated that she was scared to go inside her own apartment. A seasoned homicide detective rattled at the thought of being alone. Yeesh, what was she turning into?

"No fucking way," he ground out.

Relief rushed through her, calming frenzied nerves.

"We'll go to your apartment first, then we'll make a quick stop at the office. Whatever information is shared with me should be given to you, too. You've already been benched from doing your job. I won't let you be cut out of the investigation, too."

The conviction in his tone made her heart swell. He was treating her with the same respect as a tested partner. Similar to the bond she had with Gus, only that was where her feelings for Easton's brother stopped. The man standing in front of her, with his feet planted wide and ire flashing over his face, was a whole other story. Easton's intense eyes and warm embrace rattled her equilibrium. The rousing surge of lust that careened through her when he so thoroughly kissed her in the downstairs gym was anything but a platonic partnership.

"I appreciate it." Her words didn't even begin to explain her gratitude. "We better hit the road, then. Don't want your ass getting handed to you because of me."

"Do what you need to do. Let me worry about the rest."

Together, they walked with purpose to the side door that led to the garage. She rounded Easton's vehicle and climbed into the passenger side, then secured her seatbelt. Stealing glances at his profile had become a new favorite pastime. The lines and ridges of his face were strong and sure. His midnight eyes were framed by equally dark, thick lashes. Stubble shadowed his jawline. Clean shaven or a day's worth of scruff didn't matter— he was the most gorgeous man she'd ever laid eyes on. The SUV droned to life as the garage door cranked open behind them.

"Do you think new information was found at the coffee shop? Or another case that needs your attention?" she asked as they reversed down the driveway and straightened onto the main road.

"This is where my priority has been shifted. It'd be unlikely to get another project, given the magnitude of this case." His gaze flickered over to her before returning to the road ahead of them, and a tendril of excitement unfurled in her belly. When Easton looked at her, her breath always bottled up in her chest. His eyes were intense, and he did nothing to temper the expression of heat dancing behind the surface of his lids. "The best we can hope for is new leads."

The next twenty minutes of the ride were spent in silence, both of them scanning the traffic behind them. Nothing stood out as suspicious, but when they neared her apartment building, the white van parked out front with the name of a local nightly news channel splashed across the side made her stomach cramp.

"Dammit." Easton pounded his fist into the steering wheel. "Is there a back entrance?

"Yeah, take a left up here," she said.

Easton took the tight corner onto a side street and circled around to the rear of the property. Luck was on their side when they found an open spot near the back door. Tenants could enter the building here but rarely did. At night, the lone source of light was an eerie glow from a shattered street lamp.

"In and out. Okay?" Easton pinned her with his intense gaze.

"As soon as I throw a bag together, we're out. Not that I think anyone is lying in wait with the news van out front." She leaned forward and checked the ankle strap concealing her compact pistol and a spare magazine. When she opened the passenger door and stood, the comforting weight of the Glock Easton had loaned her was present on her hip. They both scanned the area, then strode forward. Dumpsters flanked one side of the door, and the scent of decaying fruit mixed with the metallic tang of empty soup cans hung in the air. Door hinges in need of grease squealed as she drew the door open and allowed Easton to step inside before her. The trip up the stairs to the third floor was uneventful, but she wouldn't underestimate the Kingston Town Killer. He'd taken her from a shopping center in broad daylight. It would be silly to think he wouldn't enter an apartment building. As they reached her unit, the fine hairs on the back of her neck stood, and she slowed her steps, listening for anything out of the ordinary. Easton was either hyperaware of her movements or he'd sensed it too because he stopped moving. His eyes narrowed at the base of her apartment door as he cocked his head to the side, actively listening. Her muscles tensed the longer they stood in the hallway, her heart flapping like a hummingbird caged in her chest. Then came the sound. The audible clap of shoes on the other side of her door. Easton and she exchanged a look. Someone had beat them to her apartment. Training had them each taking one side of the door. Most of the noise sounded like it was coming from the back near her bedroom. She tested the doorknob, and it rotated easily in her hands. She pushed it open, still standing against the wall instead of directly in front of the door. They'd just moved inside when a figure in dark clothing speared forward, pushing past them in an effort to leave the apartment. The intruder hit the stairs, taking them three at a time.

Adrenaline took over, and her body knew just what to do even if her brain wasn't entirely sure after these past few days. They raced after him, slamming through the glass doors at the front of the building that led to the street. The man made it down the sidewalk and was approximately twenty feet in front of him before he crumpled. They rushed up and looked down at his face where a single bullet hole marred the very center of his forehead. Someone from the news van started shouting, and Easton gripped her upper arm and dragged her into an alley.

"I'm checking for an ID." She yanked away and took a step back.

"Think about that," he hissed. "Someone cared enough to silence him, and we're damned lucky we weren't the sniper's next shot. No way you're sticking your neck out there making someone's job easy. Plus, do you want your picture on the nightly news next to the body?"

She had to make him understand, even as her throat was closing up. "We need—"

"To leave. Now." He took her hand and started to move her forward, but she dug in her heels.

Everything was spiraling out of control. Scenarios were racing through her brain, demanding her attention. "My apartment—"

"Was trashed." His hands came up to her face and stilled on her cheeks, like he was willing her to listen. To hear the words she didn't want to hear but were right. "Turned inside out. I caught a glimpse before the intruder rushed out. It wasn't pretty. As for an ID, he's not going to have one because it's doubtful he'd want to be identified if shit went south. Which it did. Now, come on. We're circling back to the car before we're next. I'll call Gus to get out here and find out what he can."

"When did you become the boss?" God, she hated how she jumped right to the defensive. Put back on all that armor when it felt as though she was losing control. It only made things worse that Easton was right about everything, and she still couldn't shake the burning frustration in her gut at the way he was taking the reins.

"When you started thinking with your emotions instead of your head? Dammit, Kinley, you're going to get yourself killed."

Shit. If that wasn't a sobering thought, she didn't know what was. Not only was she putting herself in danger, but Easton too. She wanted to apologize, but her jaw was locked in place, so she simply ground her teeth together. A gust of wind sent a crinkled trash bag rustling over the pavement. She drew her jacket more tightly around her and began to walk. Easton had already placed a call and was relaying the past fifteen minutes in a low, dangerous tone.

"A team is coming to secure the scene." He fell in line beside her. Dammit, he was using that soft cadence in his voice. Tears burned behind her lids, but she refused to let them fall. The wail of sirens echoed in the distance, and a shout was audible from the mouth of the alley. They slipped around the corner and back onto a main road. Easton's car was a welcome sight. He used his key fob to start the engine, and neither of them wasted time getting inside. The last thing they needed was a good Samaritan chasing them down with the assumption that they'd killed the man lying on the street.

"Are we good?" Easton asked. They were getting further from the city and into the suburbs.

"Depends on why you're going in the opposite direction of your office." There was a headache building behind her eyes, and she was sweltering despite the bite in the fall air.

"Plans have changed." He tapped his fingers impatiently as they slowed to a stop at a red light.

"When were you going to tell me that? I get that I came to you, but I have a problem with you calling all the shots. No, forget that. It's not just about making decisions, it's about keeping me in the dark. That's what pisses me off." She tugged off one sleeve of her coat, then the other.

He raised a brow at her before his face softened. "Shit. I'm sorry, Kins. You're right."

All the fight deflated out of her. She liked that Easton had no problem apologizing. He owned his mistakes. It was something she respected the hell out of because it was a skill she hadn't honed.

"You have no idea the control it's taking me not to throw you over my shoulder and run. Disappear where no one can hurt you. I know that makes me a chauvinistic prick, but I can't stand the thought of that bastard getting close to you. You can hold your own against any threat, but I don't want you doing it alone." He drew in a shaky breath, and for the first time, she noticed the stiffness in his shoulders and the tightly corded muscles of his neck. His drawn expression was a kick in the gut. Aside from his brother, it had been a long time since someone cared about her. "That's why we're not going to the office. Because I can't shake the thought that they were the only ones who knew we were going there aside from Gus. My brother would die before he betrayed his family, so that leaves my supervisor. It might be a fluke, but I'm not taking chances with your safety."

She was quiet for one moment, then two as she processed what he said. Maybe her instincts had been right all along. That the Kingston Town Killer was part of or was being protected by someone in law enforcement. Easton had been honest with her, and she wanted to give him the same respect.

"Ever since the day I resurrected myself from that filthy basement, I've kept everyone at arm's length." It was easier to look out the window as she spoke, but when the warmth of his right hand enveloped hers, she leaned into his touch and laced her fingers with his. She hated being touched, but not by Easton. It was unsettling how much she craved the contact of his skin against hers. "I have to call the shots, have to be in control of my own situation. If I'm not, I panic. I turn into a raging bitch. My parents got their daughter back, but I wasn't the same. No wonder they didn't feel the need to leave their lives behind and join me in New England. I wasn't mean to them, just indifferent. I couldn't connect with them. And ... and that's why it's so confusing that I want you close," she rushed out.

Heat raced up her cheeks. Yes, Gus was her partner, a friend, and she had his back, but that was where their relationship stopped. They didn't spend time together after work, nor did she accept any of Merry's invitations to hang out. Easton was different, and she couldn't deny that he was becoming important to her. He squeezed her hand. The gesture might be meaningless to some, but to her, it was a source of comfort and encouragement that gave her a surge of something more. Something that felt a lot like hope.

Chapter Ten

Easton silenced another missed call from the office as he turned down his street. Two cars were already parked out front. Gus's SUV and Kinley's car. There were things he needed to talk to Kinley about in private, but he couldn't deny it felt good that the cavalry had shown up at his door, especially given the events of the last hour. Although, now that Kinley had her car back, he'd have to talk to her about the importance of staying. Of being safe. He wasn't sure who to trust, but one thing was certain—he could always rely on his siblings to have his back.

Before he could stop the car, the garage door whipped open and Sasha jogged down the steps, bright red hair bouncing over her shoulders. She was at the passenger side door before he could kill the engine, opening the door for Kinley. Sasha wrapped Kins into a crushing hug before throwing one arm around her shoulders to walk her inside. Gus's fiancée waved at him and mouthed a hello as they rounded the car. The garage door rattled closed, and for a moment, he allowed his head to drop, his eyes to shut. That shit had been too close.

Kinley wasn't going to relive any more pain from her past. He wouldn't allow it. Yeah, right. She'd have his balls just for the mere thought of shielding her. Pain radiated through his skull, and he pinched the bridge of his nose to ease the ache. He couldn't let himself forget that the mission was to rid her and the world from the worst humanity had to offer, not interject himself into her life in a way that would hurt them both in the end. Except he couldn't wipe that kiss clean from his mind. In less than a minute, and with just one taste of her full lips, molten heat had devoured him from the inside out. And that wasn't even the dangerous part.

No, that came when the kiss tapered off, and she gave him soft and sweet. That was a direct hit to his battered soul. The way she gently nibbled on his lower lip and held on to him was his undoing. Made him wish her trauma wasn't a reflection of his own. How could he ever help her heal from what she'd been through when he wasn't truly whole himself? He released a long, jagged breath and pushed open the car door. His shoes were silent against the poured concrete, but the pulse throbbing at the base of his neck resounded in his ears. He sucked in a long breath before he climbed the three steps to the door and entered the mudroom. If he could keep his emotions in check around Kinley, he might just survive this mission.

He strode down the foyer hallway and rounded the corner. The scent was the first thing that hit him. Jules had made her famous lasagna. There was garlic bread cooling, and a half-assembled salad waited on the counter. A low growl emanated from the floor at his feet.

"Nice to see you too, Gilligan." He wasn't sure why Jules insisted on bringing that ornery chihuahua everywhere. Good thing the angry little elf was getting used to him—he'd needed stitches in the space between his thumb and index finger after their first meet and greet. His cat was probably off in some corner, stewing and plotting on the best ways to make him pay for their canine visitor. The conversation halted the moment Jules glanced up at him. She crossed the room, stood up on her toes, and threw her arms around his neck.

"Why can't my brothers ever stay out of trouble?" she whispered in his ear before releasing him. "I told Kinley to wait on updating us until we're all around the table. That way you guys only have to tell it once."

"Nothing to tell, Jules. It's an active investigation. One I want you nowhere near." His sister had witnessed enough darkness in her life. They all did their best to shelter her from the atrocities they experienced at work. The dark web was host to stomach-turning information, never mind what Gus witnessed as a homicide detective and Isaac as a SEAL.

Her lips pursed. "Thought that might be your answer. And so I'm not left feeling like the useless one in the family, there're some casseroles in your freezer."

He bent down and gave her a quick kiss on the top of her head. "You're an angel."

"Sasha and I will finish dinner while you three talk." She tipped her head toward Gus and Kinley. Gus's fiancée was slicing cucumbers and arranging them in the salad. He nodded at his sister, infusing as much appreciation as he could muster into his expression.

Gus and Kinley had crossed the room and were talking in hushed tones. As he got closer, the lines furrowing her brow and the way her hand fisted at her sides burned through his gut. He hated to see her hurting. "What's going on?" His words were sharper than he intended.

Gus raised one eyebrow, then glanced between himself and Kinley. One side of his brother's lips quirked into a smile before he neutralized his expression. Gus cleared his throat, masking the low rumble that emanated from his. Where the fuck had these protective, possessive urges bubbled up from? Isaac and Gus always described him as the laidback one, but around Kinley, he felt anything but easygoing. The rope of calm and collected ripped through his hands, no matter how tightly he tried to grasp ahold. Where she was concerned, he wanted plan on top of contingency plan. No chances. No fuckups. Not with her.

"We have some information," Gus began.

"Let's go to my office." He didn't care how many smug looks he got from Gus, the tension was shedding off of Kinley in layers so thick, it was hard to breathe past the strain in the air. He grasped her much smaller hand in his, offering his support. The way she accepted his touch though, and welcomed it, splintered something in his chest. The sharp pieces that fell away revealed something smooth and soft beneath. Something that felt a lot like contentment, or maybe even peace.

The room was located at the end of the hallway off of the living room. Originally, it had been designed as an additional main bedroom, but he'd been more than happy to fill the space with a sleek horseshoe-shaped desk with built-in cabinets lining the walls. There was a gentle hum of a hard drive cooling fan on one of numerous computers. His command center—the one place he was truly in control and could make a difference. Intel he'd uncovered during his career had led to the rescue of missing and exploited children, underage sex trafficking rings, and the prosecution of pedophiles. Yeah, he was damn proud of what he did.

Rarely did he have company in this room, but he did have a few extra chairs just in case. He dragged one of the rolling chairs away from the desk and positioned it toward Kinley.

"Thanks," she mumbled. "I'd rather stand, though. I don't think I could sit still if I tried."

"Might want to sit." Gus sighed and sank into his own chair across from her.

"That good, huh?" Kinley crossed her arms over her chest and began to pace. She was wound tight, and he hated the circumstances that caused her this angst.

He sat near the chair he'd pulled out for Kinley.

"Give it to us."

"The victim was identified by her family as Becca Murray. Multiple priors for solicitation in Worcester, Boston, and even New York. Back in the early two-thousands, though, Murray was an informant on a federal case that took down a prostitution ring in Southie. Cause of death intentional poisoning. Batrachotoxin was found in the victim's system and in the mug."

"I'll pull the names of everyone who worked that case." Maybe Becca Murray's killer had known her. Perhaps lured her to the abandoned home with the promise of compensation for new information on criminal activity.

"Batrachotoxin?" Kinley scrunched up her nose. "What the hell is that?"

"I had to look it up," Gus said. "It's a cardiotoxin and paralytic found in some frogs."

He'd already turned his chair back to the monitor to search where someone would get their hands on something like that. "Golden Dart Frogs."

"Seriously?" Kinley let out a bitter laugh. "From the great rainforests of New England? Where does that lead us?"

Easton smiled at Kinley's snark. It was so much better than hearing the pain in her voice. "Looks like you can order one online, have it shipped to you live for around eighty bucks. Highly prized among amphibian enthusiasts."

"Why do people buy pets that could potentially kill them?" Kinley quipped.

"Within minutes, according to this site." He closed the browser and angled his body toward the others.

"That's not all." Gus's tone had dropped, gone

dark. "Like the clothes, the mug was from the police barracks."

"What the ever-loving fuck?" Kinley halted in her tracks, her body turning rigid. Through the anger that had her trembling, there was fear. And that fear made acid roil in his gut.

"As much as you hate getting benched, I agree with the call to keep you off duty."

A growl of frustration tore from Kinley, and she opened her mouth to speak before Gus cut her off. "It's not safe. Whoever is doing this can get to you. Might be a person we know."

"And with that, I'll add that my supervisor was the only other person who knew we were going to the apartment today. Lora Bryce urged me to come into the office alone while Kinley got her things together. Doesn't sit right. If someone leaked that information, it's possible the intruder was lying in wait."

"No." Kinley shook her head. "We heard him before we even stepped foot in the apartment. He wasn't exactly concealing his location." She dragged her fingers through her hair and puffed out a breath.

"Maybe he thought he had more time." His brother's jaw was tight, his posture stiff. Gus looked like Easton felt. Cases were hard enough when you didn't know the victim, but when it was the woman consuming your every thought, shit got more real.

"Or he expected you to rush inside when you heard the commotion and take you out." He tried to keep his voice neutral and failed miserably.

"Then why'd he run?" Kinley stopped her pacing and spun toward him.

"Wasn't expecting me to be with you. Or we have it wrong and he was looking for something in your apartment, not someone." Damn, she was easy on the eyes. Even fired up and on edge, she knocked the wind right out of him.

"There's nothing I have. Work stays at work. I never bring files home for that very reason." Finally, she slumped in the empty chair.

"Someone paid this guy to do whatever he was doing, then was nervous enough to silence him." He gripped the arms of his chair, digging his fingers into the spongy upholstery.

There was a soft knock on the door, and Sasha poked her head in. "Lunch is ready." Gus got to his feet and stalked toward her. He palmed the back of her neck, pulling her close and kissing her deeply. A pang of envy ricocheted through him. What would it be like to be the man Kinley came home to at night? The one who could kiss her with reverence just because?

Gus glanced over his shoulder. "Let's eat. Maybe by the time we're done, we'll have an ID on the intruder." He didn't wait for a reply before following Sasha out the door.

He leaned toward Kinley and held out his hand. She placed her palm in his, studying the way their fingers linked.

"You okay?" he murmured when she didn't change the focus of her gaze.

She glanced up, eyes wide. "I … ah, I'm not used to this family-meal thing."

A warm glow spread through him. He was pleased as hell that tough-as-nails Kinley would admit to being nervous about sitting down with his family. She knew everyone, but she'd lived alone for some time now. Liked doing things on her own.

"I usually eat dinner standing at my kitchen counter," she said, confirming his thoughts.

"I get it, but even if you didn't know any of them,

they'd go out of their way to make you comfortable because you're important to me."

A pretty flush washed over Kinley's cheeks, and she absently touched her throat with her free hand. He stood, drawing her up with him. His intention had been to distract her mind from lunch, but he meant it. She was important. And now with her looking up at him with her rich maple eyes, he was the one whose attention was diverted.

The shrill ring of his phone shattered the intimate moment. He dug the device out of his pocket. Shit. He knew Bryce would be up his ass any second for not showing up at the office. Honestly, he was surprised it had taken her so long.

"Agent Adair." The frustration was audible in his tone, and Kinley bristled. "I gave you an order to report in."

Blurting out that he suspected she'd leaked their whereabouts wouldn't get him far. "And I listened to my intuition and went downtown first. I want to know what kind of criminal would make such a racket during a B&E."

"It's not your concern, Agent. You're needed in the office. You've been personally requested to provide intel on a trafficking case for another team, which I would've told you about if you came in this morning." The tapping of fingernails was broadcast over the line. A sign of his superior's displeasure.

"Whose request?" A block of ice hardened in his gut and spread, frosting his veins with panic. "And what about the task force for the Kingston Town Killer?"

"My orders come from the top, and the trafficking case has been flagged as urgent. Senator Shaw's daughter ran away from home last week, and there's reason to believe she's being groomed. I received an email from

Agent Lena Nilsson. She leads a group of five field agents in this building. She's been with the bureau for years and has an exceptional track record for these kinds of cases."

"I don't think I've ever met Agent Nilsson. There are half a dozen intelligence agents in our office alone. One of them will have to take the assignment." Thoughts and scenarios were flying through his head. "I have to go," he said abruptly and hung up the phone before Bryce could place another demand on him.

"Easton, what happened? Where are you going?" Kinley was right on his heels as he stalked out of the room and down the hall.

"Do you know Agent Nilsson?" Easton stopped in front of the dining room table and crossed his arms over his chest.

"Sure." Gus put down his salad fork. "She's worked cases we've encountered that involve children."

"She reached out to Bryce," he said. "Personally asked that I be reassigned to her group to gather intel for a trafficking case."

"Lena Nilsson?" Gus snagged a piece of bread from the basket in the center of the table. "Has to be a coincidence. She was involved with Sasha's case because Melissa Fletcher was an adolescent. Gotta say, she's the last person I'd think of who would knowingly fuck with an investigation."

"From our interactions, she seemed very by the book," Sasha volunteered.

"To the point her lack of empathy was pissing me off," Gus grumbled. "Sasha had just survived an explosion and she was at her bedside firing off questions."

"She was just doing her job, honey." Sasha put a placating hand on Gus's upper arm. His brother was damn lucky to love and be loved by a person that matched him so well. What they had was special, and for the first time in his life, Easton wondered if he was fucking up by not jumping headfirst into what was developing between him and Kinley.

"Guys, come sit and eat. Pacing around the table won't help you figure this stuff out any faster." Julie stood and grabbed the spatula from the quickly disappearing pan of lasagna. She sectioned off two huge pieces and placed one on each empty plate. "It's a freaking miracle none of you have ulcers from stress. Kins, sit next to me." She patted the seat beside her. The way his sister could deliver a polite demand, flashing her dimples and a smile, was no less effective than a drill sergeant ordering compliance. Apparently, Kinley thought so too because she slid into the chair next to Jules and picked up her fork. "I promise not to drag you off to any spas," she joked, but her smile was open and welcoming, and there was no malice in her tone.

"Between Easton's grilled cheese and now a homecooked lunch, I'm, ah … getting spoiled." She quickly pushed a lock of hair behind her ear as a blush rose up her cheek. He sat beside her and squeezed her knee. She was uncomfortable, but he wanted to kiss her senseless for engaging with his sister when there was so much stress swirling in the air.

"You're part of this crazy family whether you like it or not." Jules gave her a wink before returning to her food. He loved that his sister was welcoming Kinley into the fold.

They ate and talked, steering the topics away from the investigation for the time being. As the meal went on, Kinley's expression softened and she leaned into the table. Her smiles were no longer forced, and Jules and Sasha had them all chuckling about some recent misadventure at the grocery store. Gilligan paced under the table, occasionally stopping to paw at everyone's legs to beg for scraps. God knew Jules had most likely already fed the little sausage his own plate of noodles and sauce in the kitchen.

For the second time that hour, Easton's phone went off. The mood snapped to serious, and he silently cursed the caller for ruining the happy moment with his family. The number was one he didn't recognize.

"Hello," he said, a pit of apprehension solidifying in his chest.

"Is this Agent Adair?" the voice was female, professional, and lacking inflection.

"Yes. Who's this?" Everyone seated at the table went silent, all eyes pinned on him.

"Lena Nilsson. I'm calling to answer some questions Agent Bryce said you have about the investigation I've requested you for."

Gus shrugged and lifted his hands in a questioning gesture. Easton mouthed *Nilsson* at his brother. "I do. There are dozens of cyber-intelligence agents in our group. Why did you ask for me specifically?"

"A recommendation from Assistant Director Lenny Powers with the criminal branch. He emailed to tell me if I needed help, you were my agent. Apparently, you impressed him on a recent assignment."

Adrenaline unfurled within him, making his heartbeat quicken. "What assignment?" He pushed to his feet, no longer able to sit still.

"He didn't say." Agent Nilsson's tone remained impassive, despite his growing suspicion. "The email was brief. I just forwarded it to you." The sound of nails clicking over a keyboard sounded over the line. A second later, a ping emanated from his phone, signaling an incoming message. "Is there something I should know?"

"I've never met Powers, and I haven't worked with him on any assignments." Kinley's theory that someone in law enforcement was either the perpetrator or shielding one was seeming more viable by the minute. He fucking hated the thought that someone who had sworn to protect was hiding behind some sort of badge like a goddamn costume.

"Why would he say that, then?"

"I'm working a case that someone wants me taken off of, leaving the only known survivor of a serial killer vulnerable." He'd shared more than he intended, but Gus believed she was straight. Plus, he wanted to gauge her reaction.

"Aren't you part of the cyber division?" she asked. Christ, you'd think he'd asked what the weather forecast was based on the lack of inflection in her voice.

"There's currently some gray area." He looked fixedly at Kinley. Those big brown eyes were going to be his undoing. But the way they sparked and burned with lust when she looked at him was sweet torture.

"I see. I don't know what is going on, but I can vouch for Powers's character. He was my mentor. Has been working his whole life to put the worst of the worst behind bars."

"Well, maybe he's found some gray area himself." His eyes were still locked on Kinley's, and the way her chin was tilted upward, staring at him under her lashes, made him wonder what those pretty lips would look like wrapped around his—

"I'll reach out to someone else in your division." Agent Nilsson's clipped tone yanked him out of his fantasy. He was an asshole, plain and simple. Just because she'd allowed him to kiss her once didn't give him the right to fantasize about her when his sole mission should be protecting her. "Thank you for your transparency."

He cleared his throat. "If you get any more suspicious emails, contact me."

"Yes, I will. In fact, I'll connect with Powers. There has to be an explanation."

"As long as you know I'll still be paying him a visit." Right after he read the email Nilsson had forwarded to his inbox, he was tracking the man down.

"Naturally. I'll reach out when I make contact." Without another word, the line disconnected. The urge he had to toss Kins over his shoulder and take her upstairs to his bed hadn't subsided. He'd just have to learn to live with the permanent zipper imprint from his jeans. Now that they had a tangible lead, they had work to do.

Chapter Eleven

Lenny Powers
To: Lena Nilsson
October 23, 2021 at 10:52 PM

Lena-
Heard you could use a hand gathering intel. If you want to get this right, Easton Adair is
the agent you want. He did exceptional work with me on a recent assignment.

Lenny Powers
Assistant Director
Criminal Investigative Division

Gus read the email aloud for the second time, but Kinley's mind was focused on what Easton had been thinking of a few minutes ago when he looked at her. The thought that made his pupils dilate, darkening his eyes like a lunar eclipse. The one that made the artery jump at the base of his throat. There was a dramatic pull between them. Gravitational. Consuming. It would be some sort of miracle if she came out of this ordeal with her body and her heart unscathed. They had another piece of the puzzle where the case was concerned, but she was no closer to deciphering the feelings funneling through her when it came to Easton.

They were still sitting around the table, deciding the next steps they were going to take regarding Lenny Powers. Easton had gone to his office to trace the IP address of the server that sent the email. She'd finally relaxed and loosened up during lunch before the call came in from Agent Nilsson. There wasn't a time she could recall being so satisfied after a meal, and the ones that did pop into her head had also occurred in Easton's kitchen. Her belly was full of homecooked deliciousness, and she'd laughed out loud at Julie and Sasha's antics more than once. While she was glad to have another break in the case, she wished she'd been able to have a few more moments of normalcy with Easton's family.

"Sent from a computer located at his home address." Easton spoke as he entered the kitchen. "Look at the date and time. October twenty-third was a Saturday, and he didn't send the email until nearly eleven o'clock at night."

"Let's go." Gus pressed a kiss to his fiancée's temple, then stood up and rounded the table.

"I'm coming, too." She took the napkin off her lap and placed it on the table.

"Kinley, it'd be better if you stayed." A frown darkened Gus's face.

Damn, that stung. Her partner was cutting her out of the investigation. Sasha rolled her striking blue eyes and crossed her arms over her chest. She appreciated the other woman's support. Gus was lucky to find her— brave, beautiful, and bold enough to call Kinley's partner on his crap.

"Like hell." Her hands automatically went to her hips. "I'm going. If you have an issue with that maybe you should stay behind."

There was a low grumble to her left. "She can handle herself."

Kinley did a double take as surprise fluttered in her belly. Easton had mirrored her stance and was staring at Gus with a pissed-off scowl. He had her back, and that filled her with a warm, hazy glow. She was losing her edge. Swooning over Easton would only hurt her in the end. She'd been alone for so long, she didn't know how to be in a relationship. If she screwed things up, she'd hate herself for it.

"'Course, I can. How many times have I gotten your sorry ass out of a jam?"

Gus flinched even as the corner of his lip twitched.

"Meet you outside." She had walked past them both in the direction of the garage.

"Didn't say she couldn't handle her shit," she heard Gus saying to Easton. "But she's like a little sister. We could be walking into a cluster."

"But she's not. Give your partner a little credit and stop looking at her like a victim." Easton's words warmed her. He started to say something else, but the sound was muffled when she closed the door behind her. She got in the front seat and waited. The door swung open a few seconds later, and both men made their way to the car. Gus opened the door and slid into the back seat behind Easton, who slammed his door and started the engine.

"Sorry for being a dick. I was out of line," Gus's voice was sincere, and she looked over her shoulder to face him. "You've never given me any reason not to trust your ability. I want to shield you from this and shoulder some of the weight you always carry alone. You saved my woman's life. My entire world. No matter what happens, you are part of this family. You don't have to go it alone anymore."

A lump formed in her throat, blocking off her words. How'd she get so lucky to find these people? Maybe it was time to accept that having a support system didn't make her weak. It made her human. She'd been on autopilot for a long time because it was easier than feeling. Easton had dissolved that barrier though, and emotions she'd boxed up and locked down tight were flooding to the surface. She turned in her seat, unable to offer a response to her partner's kindness.

Easton had plugged an address into his GPS and was backing out of the driveway. Instead of going toward the city, they traveled deeper into suburbia to a gated community in a wealthy town in Middlesex County.

Easton pulled the car up to the gatehouse, and a security guard opened the glass partition.

"Good afternoon. Name and identification, please." The cuff of the man's starched white shirt rose up as he reached for Easton's driver's license.

"Easton Adair, Kinley Wright, and Gus Lambert here to see Lenny Powers."

The guard dipped his chin and scanned his clipboard. "Sorry, you're not on the visitor's list."

"We're here on official business." Easton produced a leather billfold and held it out to the guard. The man's brow furrowed as he leaned in to look at the gold badge and identification.

"One moment." The guard closed the window and picked up a telephone. After a minute, the glass slid open again. "Mr. Powers is available to see you." Without any additional pleasantries, the gate opened, and they drove slowly down the private road lined with sprawling Cape Cod-style homes.

"This is it." Easton turned into a two-story home with natural shingled siding. They exited the car and walked up the stone steps leading to the central front door. Before they had a chance to knock, a fit, middle-aged man opened the door.

"Just got off the phone with Agent Nilsson. I was expecting you to stop by. Come in. We can talk in the living room." Powers led them past the kitchen and gestured toward the large sectional. "Take a seat."

"I'd like to know more about the email you sent

Agent Nilsson and why." Easton cut right to the chase as he sat down beside her.

"I have the same questions." The man sat across from them in a floral-printed accent chair.

"Do you deny sending it? The email came from an IP address at this location," Easton said.

For a man whose intentions were being questioned, and by someone of a lower rank, he was quite calm. "I do." Powers scrubbed his hand over his cheek. "I certainly wasn't sending emails on Saturday night."

"What were you doing?" she asked. There was more bite in her tone than she intended.

"My wife and I hosted a dinner party." He glanced down at his clasped hands, then back at her. "The last guests went home around midnight."

"We'll need a list of everyone who was here."

"Of course." He stood up and patted his pockets. "Let me get a pen and I'll jot down some names." He crossed the room and opened the top drawer of a decorative cabinet positioned against the back wall, then returned to his armchair. "I'm taking this seriously. I consider every guest a close friend, and it burns me to think someone took advantage of being in my home. Once you leave, I'll be reporting this breach to the bureau."

"Are you familiar with the Kingstown Killer case?" Easton didn't have to yell or shout to get across the gravity of his anger. She couldn't be the only person in this room to feel it shimmering off him in waves.

The man's head jerked back, and his brow furrowed. "I don't know an agent who isn't. You think that email has something to do with that case?"

"That's exactly what we think."

"Please explain, because I don't think I'm

following." Powers's view flashed to her, and realization dawned over his face. "Christ. Little Kinley Miller. That's you, isn't it?"

In the past few days, she had heard her parents' last name repeatedly. Those two syllables had been plastered over every Sunday newspaper at the time of her disappearance, and she'd be content never hearing them again. Kinley ground her teeth together.

Janie. Janie. Janie.

"Kinley." Easton's sharp bark made her mind snap to the present. He held her gaze for one breath, then two. His dark eyes grounded her, making her feel stronger than she actually was.

"Wright. Now, my last name's Wright." She projected a false bravado, and even though her voice quivered, she was proud she wasn't shaking. "I came here to blend."

Powers leaned forward in his chair. "So when the nightly news said you shared your story..."

"Never happened." Even though the state police had connected with the local television channels to pull the story, it had gained too much momentum.

"I'm sorry you're having to relive this, then," Powers said in a soft voice.

"Not as sorry as we are." Gus leaned forward, resting his elbows on his knees. "We're going to review this list, and will be in touch if any questions come up."

"Good luck to you." Powers nodded and stood up. "I'll make my team aware of what's happening, and I hope to God no one with nefarious intentions was seated at my table. You better believe we'll fetter out whoever sent that email from my home."

They stood and followed Powers to the door, then took the stone steps to the driveway. They got into the vehicle with more questions than answers. Behind them, tires squealed over the pavement, followed by a rapid succession of gunfire. Shit. As the back window exploded, Kinley ducked her head and grabbed her weapon.

"Gus!" She wrenched around in her seat. Her partner had drawn his gun and crouched down.

"Fuck! Go, just go!" Blood dripped from the shards of glass embedded in Gus's skin, but otherwise, he appeared unscathed.

The seatbelt went taut around her, stealing her breath as Easton accelerated. More shots rang out, this time deployed from their backseat. They fish-tailed, tires grinding against asphalt until they gained traction. The scent of burned rubber seeped through the vents. She was thrust forward, the seatbelt pressed against her sternum with crushing force as the car tailing them slammed into their bumper.

"Dammit!" Gus roared from the back. She glanced up at Easton, who was laser focused on the road in front of them. He was silent as he maneuvered the vehicle with precision.

"The gatehouse," she murmured and holstered her weapon at her hip, grappling for her cell phone instead.

"Call it in," Easton said. The windows of the security checkpoint were shot out, and the guard who had greeted them less than an hour ago was sprawled out on the pavement with twin spots of blood seeping through his stark shirt. She'd already dialed nine-one-one and began relaying the information. The car was right on their ass, swerving around traffic to catch up as they hit the main road. Instead of staying on the line with the first responder as requested, Kinley disconnected and dropped the phone into the center console.

"Coming up on your left," she shouted as the car built momentum. Her heart was beating double time, and the back of her neck was soaked in sweat. "Do you think Powers is behind this? He could've tipped someone off with a quick text."

The passenger in the other vehicle raised his semi-automatic. Easton hit the gas, pushing the car to the limit. She lost sight of black ski masks and leather gloves but was lurched to the side, metal grinding on metal as the cars pushed together. "Possible. Or someone followed us." Easton veered into the right shoulder lane, then cut the wheel, slamming hard against their aggressors. The car slowed, but it wasn't enough.

"Which means they might know where you live." Gus bit out.

No one had followed them out of Easton's street. She was sure of it. If not the house though, where and how had they located them?

The windows on the driver's side blew out, showering them with glass. She lifted her hands to protect her head, then the window behind Easton shattered with a deafening blast. Icy wind snaked into the car from the smashed glass, freeing fragile shards that clung to the frames.

A particle nicked her cheek, and warm drips of blood dotted her pants. "Bastards." Anger flared in her chest. She hit the release on her seatbelt and turned, shifting to her knees.

"Kinley, no!" Easton's voice was louder than she'd ever heard it, fury and fear melding into one force. "Sit down and buckle up. Goddamn, you're gonna get killed."

She ignored his outburst, gripping the cool metal stock of her firearm. With most of the windows removed, she had a clear shot. Aiming out the back, she pulled the trigger. Once. Twice. A third time for good measure. The driver slumped forward and skidded into the guardrail.

Horns blared around them. She gave the assailants one final glance. The hood of their car had crushed like an empty soup can and both airbags had deployed.

She flipped the safety on her gun and eased down into her seat.

"Well done, Annie Oakley," Gus praised.

"Are you out of your fucking mind?" Easton lost his cool. "That was reckless." He punched the wheel with such force that she recoiled. "Don't ever pull that shit again. Ever, Kinley." The car fell into a stony silence, tension thickening in the space between them.

"If she hadn't—" Gus began.

"Don't say it," Easton said with a growl.

"Get your head out of your ass." Gus threw his hands up. "If she wasn't your woman, you wouldn't be on the verge of a shit fit."

His woman?

She was supposed to be independent. A hardened homicide detective. Kinley belonged to no one. Not now, not ever. Damned if the insinuation didn't feel good, though.

Easton glared at Gus through the review mirror, and the scowl that marred his face would've been comical if it weren't for the harrowing high-speed chase.

The only words spoken for the remainder of the ride were when Gus called Sasha and Jules to check in before contacting the barracks to fill them in on the situation. Later, they'd have to give a statement to the FBI. They circled and backtracked for over an hour to make sure they didn't have a tail, and they didn't return to Easton's house until after dark.

When the garage rumbled shut, the door to the house flew open. Gus had barely exited the car before Sasha leaped into his arms. "Oh, my God. What hurts the worst?" His fiancée's eyes were wide as she surveyed his bloodied face. She rushed him inside, one hand on his back and the other on his shoulder. Gus might tower over Sasha in size, but what the woman lacked in stature, she sure made up for in guts.

"Stay there." Easton's hoarse voice was barely a whisper. He yanked the door open, dislodging some of the loose shards of glass from the window sill. Too close. She could've lost them both. Easton stalked around the hood, his face like granite. She only had time to unbuckle before he was reaching down and hauling her up. His eyes, nearly black now, held a hurricane of emotion rioting in the depths. She wasn't able to decipher what he was feeling before his mouth collided with hers. His hands fisted in her hair, angling her head right where he wanted it. "Scared me," he murmured against her lips. "Fucking hell, Kins." He drove back into the kiss, and she met him stroke for stroke, devouring him, needing more. He'd been frightened for her. While she felt bad he'd been alarmed, his concern made her feel cared for. Their tongues clashed in a desperate dance. One of Easton's hands released her hair and looped around her waist, holding her flush against him. The car's cold metal frame was at her back as he pinned her in place. Liquid heat built in her belly and gathered at the junction of her hips. When he nipped her bottom lip, a guttural sound tore from her throat. His lips traveled down her jaw. Goosebumps broke out over her body as his hot breath tickled her skin. "Promise." His desperate words were muffled by the kisses he pressed against the sensitive curve of her nape. "No more chances." Wetness seeped from her core. For the second time in twenty-four hours, Easton's hard length was pressed against her.

"Easton." Mind-numbing lust had made her voice raw, vulnerable.

"Baby, swear it." When his tongue circled her

earlobe, she felt it everywhere. Overwhelming sensations lit up her skin from the top of her head to her toes. How could she possibly deny him anything?

"Promise," she whispered and rocked her hips against him. His sharp gasp emboldened her. There were no lies she could tell herself anymore. Everything about Easton resonated in the unexplored, untouched places inside her heart. She was drawn to him in a way she never imagined possible. The fact that they were standing in his garage, that the others were right inside the house, failed to register. The only thing that mattered was stopping this hollow ache. She slipped her hands beneath his shirt, exploring the taut muscles of his stomach and the lines of his hips. Her fingers fumbled with the button of his jeans, and he sucked in a breath and stilled.

"Fuck. I lost myself there." He lowered his forehead to hers, and for a moment, they just stood against the car, connected. The feeling wasn't just sexual—it roamed past physical to the unexplored wild of her soul.

"I wouldn't object if you want to lose yourself again." She smiled, shocking herself by teasing him at such an intense moment. He made her feel lighter, happier.

There was a brisk knock on the door before it opened a crack. "Don't mean to interrupt, but you need to get in here." The seriousness of Gus's tone was enough to get her body under control. The cold trickle of dread ate up all the lovely warmth Easton infused. Was her life always destined to be that way? A sick twist and tug between torture and bliss?

Chapter Twelve

"What happened?" Easton looked over the granite island to Gus and tightened his grip on Kinley's hand. When she moved closer to him, he knew with soul-deep clarity he would give his life to protect her. He'd long ago acknowledged that the horrible abuse he'd endured didn't make him less of a person, but that didn't mean he was unscathed. He was a splintered bone that never fused back the same way. A wound that refused to scab. The memories were always there, waiting until he least expected them to slam into his chest. The pain so acute and fresh, nothing ever seemed to dull the sensation. Until Kinley. Her strength fortified his own, and something unexpected soothed the old lesions. Happiness. His innocence might've been taken, but what he did with his future, the love and happiness he experienced, was his alone.

"The coroner identified the intruder at Kinley's apartment." Gus placed both hands on the edge of the counter. "Marshall Redding. Twenty-six. Low-level security guard from Oasis Renewable Energy."

"That's directly across from the bureau's office," he said.

Kinley inhaled a sharp breath. "If he was unhappy with his situation, it wouldn't take much for someone to sway him to take a side job. Extra cash, a real piece of the action."

"Especially if the person doing the convincing carried their own badge and security clearance." Gus pressed his lips together in a grim line.

A loud chime echoed through the room, catching all three of them off guard. Kinley let out a huff and rolled her eyes. "Guess we're all wound up tight." She let go of his hand to grab the device from her pocket, and the loss of the physical connection hit him immediately. "It's a text from Merry, the dispatcher at work. She found something." Her fingers flew over the small letter icons, the screen illuminating her pretty face.

I was walking to my car and noticed a note on the cruiser you drive. No one's taken it out since the homicide.

I saw your story on the news last night and was worried.

I brought the message inside to the lieutenant.

Kinley sent the message she'd typed out, even as her phone kept ringing with incoming texts. **What did it say?**

Almost immediately, the other woman responded. **Soon.**

He'd been expecting Kinley's fear, but instead, her face twisted in anger.

Maybe I'm overreacting. It wasn't even addressed to you, but I wanted to give you a head's up. You're the most fearless woman I know. I'm so sorry for all you went through.

Kinley's neck and chest reddened, and he swore she bared her teeth. She snapped out another text and hit send.

Who was it for?

A moment passed, then another. Kinley was staring at the screen of her phone while Gus and he exchanged concerned looks. The phone pinged, and she read the text. Tightness formed around her eyes. She angled the phone toward him, then Gus, so they could both read the message.

Someone named Janie.

Anger roiled in his gut, digging and clawing, desperate for vengeance. "How well do you know this woman?"

"Merry?" She tossed down the phone, and the hard plastic case clattered on the stone surface. "Christ, she's not only trustworthy, she's an angel. Plus, she's no threat. Makes Sasha look tall. The only harm she's ever inflicted is a few inches around the hips with all the treats she spoils us with."

"Heard that," Sasha yelled from the living room where she and Julie were watching television on the couch.

"The point is, Merry is not involved." Kinley angled her body toward him, resting one elbow on the counter.

"I'd have to agree with Kinley on this one." Gus stepped back and crossed his arms over his chest. "Although..."

"What?" He didn't want them missing even the smallest detail because they were friendly with the dispatcher.

"Her father's FBI," Gus said. "Retired, so maybe it's a stretch. But you did mention you thought there was a leak. Maybe he still has access to information through friends."

"He was a decorated agent." Kinley rolled her shoulders. "It's not him. I'd know. The voice, it's not right. Merry's dad has a deep baritone and brown eyes. The man who took me... I'll never forget the high pitch of his voice. Or his eyes. This terrible milky blue."

His stomach churned at the thought of Kinley being violated. He shoved his emotions away and focused. "What if he was protecting someone?"

"Shit." Gus rubbed his hand over his mouth. "He's at the barracks a helluva lot."

Kinley sighed. "Delivering coffee to Merry. He hardly snoops around."

"But he's buddies with the lieutenant. Everyone's used to seeing him around." Gus flashed Kinley a pointed look.

"I guess I wouldn't think twice if he was grabbing a mug from the kitchen." She shrugged.

"If I noticed him taking dry cleaning out of the closet, I'd just assume it was for Merry." Gus pinched the bridge of his nose.

"Okay, so what if he has access? Why would a celebrated agent commit murder, then dress the victim to look like me?"

"To send you a warning." It was the only logical explanation he could think of at the moment, but it just didn't make sense.

"Initially, that's what I was thinking too, but it's not like Kinley has been searching for her abductor. She's not a threat." Gus lifted his arms and dropped them to his sides. "If someone was afraid of her discovering the killer's identity, why dredge all this shit up with an email? Why all the theatrics?"

"Gus is right. It would make more sense to kill me and silence me for good."

Christ, he hated that she could talk about her death so clinically. He couldn't stomach it. "Let's do some digging on the father."

"What's going on with the task force for the case?" Gus said.

"A current trafficking case has taken precedence." Pain radiated through his clenched jaw. "Senator Shaw's daughter might be involved. The satellite office closest to Hunt County is investigating."

"Most of the victims were found in that general location. It makes sense a task force would be created there, too." Her expression was drawn, and he wanted nothing more than to scoop her up, take her to his bed, and tuck her beneath his sheets.

"I need to contact Bryce and have her reassign my workload for the week. Looks like this is our task force right now. Let's not waste any more time before going through Powers's guest list."

"I'll bring in some sandwiches." Jules had quietly padded into the kitchen, her sloth socks muffling the sound of her movements.

"Thanks." Although Julie was the youngest, she'd taken on a nurturing role in foster care. She was always fussing over them, and they loved her for it. She was the glue to their family.

Kinley took his hand as they started down the hall. Today had been a clusterfuck, but he still found himself drawing in a long, contented breath. He loved how she reached out to him for comfort, even in front of Gus. The skin-to-skin contact calmed him in ways he didn't fully comprehend. One thing was certain though—having her close made him question the future he'd imagined for himself. A life that didn't involve a family outside the one forged with his siblings. Certainly not a woman to care for, to share a life with. He never thought he'd have the desire after the hell his mother put him through. But Kinley had a way of making him feel like he could conquer anything.

It was more than just recognizing another survivor. It was like identifying a broken piece of himself, one he knew with terrifying clarity would snap perfectly into place if given a chance. The Kingston Town Killer's days were numbered. Kinley was his, and he'd never stop hunting until she was safe.

Chapter Thirteen

"Who's next on the list?" Easton asked in between bites of a turkey sandwich. He swiveled his chair, fingers poised over the keyboard, waiting for one of them to call out another name. Easton was at the large monitor, while she and Gus flanked him on either side.

"Tina and Roger Moss," Gus said, reaching over Easton to grab another sandwich from the tray Jules prepared for them.

"Mrs. Moss teaches private piano lessons, and Mr. Moss works in accounting at the bureau. Nothing of note in either one of their histories." Easton rocked back in the seat and placed both hands on top of his head. "Unless Powers is fucking with us, someone on that list sent us the email."

Kinley stood and walked over the list. She peered over Gus's shoulder, reading down the names. They had about five more to investigate.

"Just got an email from Powers," Easton said, minimizing one tab and opening another. "His team is dusting his office for fingerprints."

Kinley's finger paused on one of the names scrawled on the list. "Not gonna find anything."

"Maybe there's a partial somewhere." Gus held up the tray, offering her another sandwich, and she waved him away. There was no way she could eat with her stomach clenching in painful knots. How had she missed it the first time she'd skimmed the list?

"There won't be." Kinley crossed her arms over her chest. Perhaps Easton's instincts had been right where Merry was concerned, but she hated to think of someone so bright and pure having immoral intentions. "If this individual is who I think it is," she said tapping her index finger on the paper. "He would've taken precautions. Pros at his level don't slip up."

"Who?" Easton turned to face her.

She liked how he didn't question her hunch. He trusted her, and damn if it didn't feel good to have his respect. "Maxwell Calder."

"Fuck." Gus sat up straight and leaned in to look at the list.

"Someone fill me in." Easton rubbed his eyes with the heels of his hands and refocused on the paper.

"The dispatcher who texted me. Her last name is Calder. I don't know Merry's father's first name, but what are the odds?"

Easton turned back to his keyboard and began typing in the name. Within seconds, pictures of Merry's father, retired agent Calder, filled the screen. "Moved here in two thousand and sixteen. Give me a sec to pull up his property records. Purchased a home on Lake Boon in Hudson. Less than thirty minutes from the barracks."

The ringing in her ears drowned out the sound of Easton's voice. Her chest was tight, the room too small. A strong grip vised around her arm.

"Kins," Easton barked. He was inches from her, face hard and drawn. The moment she focused on him instead of the impending panic attack, his features softened and he tugged her into his side. "Don't fight it. Trying to stop or deny it only makes them worse. Breathe through it with me."

He dropped slowly to his knees, still anchoring her in his embrace, and sat on the floor against the wall. Easton maneuvered her onto his lap, so his solid chest was to her back. When he inhaled, long and deep, his ribcage rose against her spine, and she automatically drew in her own breath. For fifteen minutes, they sat on the floor of the office. She kept glancing at the clock on the wall, relieved and humbled that Easton didn't try to rush the process of going back to their search just yet. He seemed to know instinctively what she needed. He didn't rub her back or whisper soothing words. Easton simply circled his arms around her lower waist and locked her against him like a safety belt. He breathed and held on as her heart drilled like a fully automatic unloading a thirty-round magazine. Twice in a matter of two days, Easton witnessed her struggling. He didn't make her feel weak. He made her feel like a fighter.

At some point, Gus had exchanged a silent look with Easton and gave them privacy. As her pulse evened out, she glanced at the clock once more. Half an hour. Frustration hit her square in the gut. Time they should've been formulating a plan to uncover more about Maxwell Calder.

"Don't go there, Kins." Easton's breath caressed her shoulder.

"What do you mean?" She leaned her head back against his chest, giving him more of her weight. She'd been doing that a lot lately. Letting Easton shoulder some of the burden. Shouldn't have made her feel so cared for, but it did.

"You're looking at the clock, wondering about wasted time. You're not a machine. We've been on edge all day. Sitting on this floor, breathing, regulating, is exactly where we need to be at this moment."

"Thank you," she murmured, not quite sure how to say it meant the world for him to understand on such an intimate level.

"Don't have to thank me for taking care of you. It feels as natural as breathing." Now that she was no longer in the midst of a panic attack, she was aware of how well they fit together. His fresh scent filled her nostrils, and she did everything she could to coat her lungs with it. To memorize it because nothing had ever smelled sexier.

An involuntary sigh escaped her lips, blowing up a strand of her hair. As much as she never wanted Easton to let her go, it was time to work. She scooted off of his lap and got to her feet. The panic attack had made her queasy and weak, not that she'd let Easton know. "I'll call Gus back in."

"No need." He tilted his head slightly, looking up at her with an expression that made her already overloaded heart skip a beat.

"Why?"

"He went home with Sasha." Easton ran both hands down his heavily muscled thighs. Ones that filled out his jeans quite nicely. "Julie left too," he said, and she tore her gaze away from his lower half. "Gus is taking over the research for a few hours so we can rest."

"But—" she protested.

"But nothing. We have your back. We're a team, and we work like one. Let's go to bed, Kins. I want you tucked into me safe and warm."

Her body hummed, not seeming to register that Easton was only talking about sleeping. "I don't know if that's quite what I had in mind."

"If you need that release, baby, you'll get it." His voice dropped, gruff and thick with need. "With my tongue, my fingers. I'll lick and suck every inch of your beautiful body. Just know, when I'm inside you, there will be no one else in our bed. Just me and you, Kins. I won't let you get lost in the shadows. That darkness isn't allowed to enter your head when I'm loving you."

She couldn't help the spontaneous moan at his crass words. Loved hearing them spoken from his lips. And she couldn't deny the swoony feeling in her belly when he used the words *our bed*. The darkness and the shadows flitting through her mind were not what she'd be thinking of when Easton was inside of her. Her head would be somewhere much more dangerous. It had only been a few days, yet her heart was inexplicitly, wholly focused on the man still sitting on the floor, patiently waiting for her next move.

He was good, straight down to the marrow of his bones. Protecting, encouraging, and making her feel beautiful and wanted instead of dirty and disgraced. He could light her up with just one hungry look or embolden her with his praise. Of course, when he snapped at her in the car for getting rid of the tail, it was annoying as all get out. But no one had ever cared about her well-being so much before. She turned and reached down, offering her hands. He took them but stood easily on his own. Kind of like how she was feeling right now. Easton was teaching her that just because she was one hundred percent capable of being on her own, she didn't have to be. That steadying hand waiting to offer help didn't make her pathetic or fragile. It made her human. Not the robot she'd been trying to impersonate for so long.

With Easton standing, she looked up and swallowed hard at the lust-driven look consuming his eyes. Their hands were still linked, and she took a step closer. "I swear when we come together, the only thing I'll be thinking of is how strong and wanted you make me feel. How perfectly you fill me up. How I know once will never be enough."

"God damn, Kins." His fingers trembled as he released her hands and brought them to her face. He cupped her cheeks so gently, heat prickled behind her lids. "So fucking gorgeous. You keep knocking me flat on my ass. I'm in awe, baby. So brave." He pressed a kiss to her forehead. "So resilient." His lips moved down to the tip of her nose. The kiss he placed there was the sweetest gesture anyone had ever shown her.

She shut her eyes, savoring the gentleness he was offering.

"Compassionate. Despite everything, you fight for others." He kissed her left eyelid. "My gladiator." And then his lips feathered over her right eyelid. She couldn't stop the tear from slipping down her cheek if she wanted to, but she didn't. Easton deserved to see her. Raw, exposed, and vulnerable. He laid his emotions out at her feet, and he deserved no less.

"I'm scared. But it's not why you think." Her voice was merely a whisper. The steady stream of autumn sunshine had turned to dusky shadows playing over the walls, but she wasn't scared of the dark. Not with Easton at her side.

"Then why don't you explain?" His fingers skimmed over her jawline, down to her shoulders.

"It's insane." She forced herself to meet his eyes. "To feel this way so fast. I'm afraid of what I'm feeling for you. That once this is all over and we go our separate ways, you'll take my heart with you and I'll be crushed. I've never even come close to saying those three words to someone. Never thought it was possible. But with you, after such a short time, they're on the tip of my tongue, and I'm not sure how I'm going to get through losing you." Her words came out in a whoosh before she dropped her forehead to his chest. What had he been saying about brave and resilient? Yeah, right. She was shocked by how transparent she was with him, and yet, she didn't want to take anything she said back.

"Why do you think you'll lose me?" He moved his forehead against hers, once again tethering them.

"Because … I … I'm not built for relationships or long-term. I'll screw up or get scared and try to push you away. You'll realize I have way too many issues to be worth your time. I don't want kids. You deserve a family, someone without so many demons—"

"That right there is complete and utter bullshit. You're not built for relationships? Well, neither am I, but I have a feeling with you, we could lay a strong foundation, build something lasting. If you push me away, I'll hold tighter. And kids? What makes you think I want them? Let's leave that headache to Gus and Sasha. I have a cat. Would love to get a couple of dogs to leave their muddy paw prints over the floor. I love the idea of being an uncle. Help my siblings raise good humans, but I have no desire to have children and there's nothing wrong with that. Kids can make a family whole, but a family can also be whole without them. Having people by your side, who have your back when shit goes sideways, that's family all on its own. The one we're born into or the one we discover along the way, it doesn't matter. Neither is better or worse. And last and most important, you will always be worth my time. I'm not looking for a quick, meaningless fuck. No woman has ever stepped foot in this house. I can't predict what will happen between us, but I do know I will never hurt you." With a light touch, he lifted her chin. "Do you trust me?"

"Yes." The word popped out of her mouth without an instant of hesitation. The only other person she had nearly as much faith in was Gus, and he'd been her partner for years. Part of her simply settled when Easton was near. He'd never let anything or anyone touch her, and without a doubt in her mind, she'd have his back, too.

He nuzzled her neck, the day-old stubble on his cheeks and chin sending prickles of pleasure over her skin. "Let's go up to bed, then." He tucked a wayward strand of hair behind her ear. "Whatever you want, I'll give it. Whatever you don't, tell me, and that's as far as things will go. No matter what, you're in control."

He took her hand, and they made their way to the second floor, except this time, instead of going toward Julie's room, Easton led her directly to his bedroom. The scent of the soap he used lingered in the air, making her feel protected. He closed the door behind them and stalked forward.

"So fuckin' beautiful, Kins." His hands went to her face, thumbs slowly stroking the lines of her cheeks. She loved when he touched her so reverently like she was some kind of treasure. And the way his pupils dilated, eyes turning into inky pools, so dark that her reflection was mirrored clearly in their depths. She'd never get sick of hearing her name on his lips. Or how he always thought of her perception of a situation. He had no problem laying himself bare to ensure she was aware of his intentions and feelings.

He leaned down and kissed her, nibbling on her bottom lip and dipping his tongue into her mouth. When she planted her hands on his chest, his heart thundered against her palms. His hands slid into her hair, angling her head to delve deeper. With every thrust of their tongues, a new sensation consumed her. Each time her nipples brushed against the satin cups of her bra, it was torture. Wetness pooled between her thighs, and anticipation hummed from somewhere deep in her throat.

He paused for a moment, searching her face. His hands dropped from her hair and slipped beneath the hem of her shirt, warming her back. "This okay?" His body was vibrating, heat tumbling off of him, but what melted her from the inside out was his sole focus. Her. Paying attention to what she wanted. As much as she couldn't wait to feel his control snap, the care he was taking was so perfectly Easton. This was who he was. One of the many reasons she was losing her heart to him.

"More." She had a feeling he wouldn't move a muscle until she told him she was ready.

"Like this?" he asked, hands skimming up her sides. He paused before removing her shirt. She nodded, goosebumps shivering up her skin as cool air replaced the fabric. With trembling fingers, he unclasped her bra and let it fall to the floor. Impatient for more, she pushed down her jeans and panties before realizing she was tangled. Easton chuckled and dropped down, skimming his hands down the back of her legs as he sank to the floor. With a hand behind her knee, he lifted her right leg and removed her bunched clothing from around her ankle before moving to the other.

He stood and took a long look at her, the hunger flitting across his face now ravenous. "Stunning." His voice was a hoarse whisper, choked with heat.

She reveled in being the one to put the passion in his voice, on his face. "Why am I the only one naked here?" She grinned at him, comfortable in her own skin, and stepped closer to tug up his shirt. He ripped it over his head before shucking off his pants and boxers, kicking them to the side. Kinley unabashedly took him in. He was sculpted with lean muscle and hard lines from his broad shoulders to strong thighs. His erection long and thick. There was a weightless feeling in her stomach. One that made her body clench and her breasts grow heavy.

In one graceful movement, he scooped her up. She squealed in surprise, which dissolved into laughter. She couldn't remember a time where she was so happy and light. Probably never, which was crazy given the danger she was in.

He gently laid her on the bed and crawled in beside her, the soft mattress depressing slightly with their weight. Her blood was heated, and he hadn't even touched her skin. She'd never felt like this. Not ever. Their lips touched once, then twice, before his tongue slipped into her mouth, and they both groaned. His hands were on her, spreading white-hot tingles wherever he touched. When he plumped her breasts and rolled the stiff peaks between his fingers, heat careened through her. Needing more, she lifted her hips, seeking more friction to ease the building ache. With his hands stuck to her sides, he flipped them in one fluid movement so she was sitting astride him.

"So damn beautiful," he murmured, gathering the wetness from her core and circling her clit. A shiver of pleasure raced down her spine. "Move up, baby." His hands worked over the flare of her hips, sliding her body up and over his mouth. She grabbed the headboard, totally unprepared as he dragged his tongue over her sex. The growl that tore from his lips vibrated against her. He licked and teased until she was writhing over him, mind blank to any embarrassment over her precarious position. "You taste so fucking good," he groaned. More pleasure rippled as he stretched two fingers inside her, curling them slightly and hitting a place she didn't even know existed. His lips latched on to her clit and sucked hard. She screamed, white knuckles gripping the frame as she broke into a million pieces. His tongue kept moving in lazy strokes as she came down from her orgasm.

"Easton, I want more. All of you." She began to move back, but his hands on the back of her thighs stopped her progress.

"Tasting you come apart on my tongue, feeling you shake... Fuck, it was incredible. I could tuck you against me right now and be completely satisfied. We don't need to go any further."

"As I said, all of you." She didn't need to ask if he wanted more. Easton was holding on by a thread. His grip loosened and she crawled back, positioning his tip at her entrance. "Skin to skin. I don't want a barrier between us."

"You know I would never put you at risk. I've been tested. I'm clean, so—" He sucked in a breath as she dropped down, taking all of him. Years had passed since she'd been with someone, but he'd made sure she was slick and ready. Just another way Easton had put her first. They moved together, eyes locked, hands intertwined. Connected. He filled her so completely, body and soul, there was no room for shadows. No room for darkness. No room for anything but Easton and her and how they fit together like the jagged pieces of a shattered vase.

Chapter Fourteen

Easton had been awake for a while, soaking in the feeling of Kinley's body tangled around him. The night before had been nothing less than earth-shattering. Now her bare back was against his chest, his arms firmly wrapped around her waist, their legs tangled together. This was exactly what he wanted. What he'd fight for. Maybe he'd been in denial all along, but after last night, hearing every sweet sigh, feeling every tremble, he was lost in the heaven that was his woman. His. Kinley owned his heart, and he didn't want it back. The rise and fall of her breath echoed against his skin, and the sweet scent of her hair enveloped him. All his life, he'd been fighting his past, going through the motions of the present, but now, for the first time, he was excited about the future. About all the things he wanted to experience with Kinley.

They needed to talk, though. It was his responsibility to keep her safe, and right now, he was doing a shit job of it. Diving into bed with her took his focus off of the case. Instead of patrolling the perimeter and scouring the internet for more information, he'd been lost to her. How could he live with himself if his feelings ended up affecting his work so much that Kinley was killed?

His phone rang, and he cursed under his breath. He gently released Kinley and turned to his nightstand.

He glanced at the phone and frowned. "'Ello?" Easton swung his legs over the side of the bed, bypassed the clothing strewn over the floor, and stalked into the bathroom.

"Adair." His superior's voice filled the line. "I received your message and spoke with Agent Powers.

You have your taskforce. The District Attorney has granted us a search warrant for Maxwell Calder's home. The state police got a hit on the partial print found at the scene of the homicide on Highland Path. Agent Nilsson has requested to assist, and Powers will be stepping in on the trafficking situation. You also have agents Eliza Brigham and Tyler Dawson. Let's bring him in for questioning. I've arranged for a temporary vehicle to be dropped off at your location. Two agents should be pulling into your driveway at any moment. After all these years, we might have our first person of interest in the Kingston Town Killer case."

"Thank you. Happy to have Nilsson and the others on this. I'll report in to the office right away." After the call was disconnected, he turned on the shower and stepped inside, too impatient to wait while the water warmed. He took what his brother would call a military shower, soaping up and rinsing off in record time. When he walked out of the bathroom, a towel slung around his hips, Kinley was sitting up in bed. She'd tossed on one of his t-shirts while he'd been in the shower, and damn, he loved the look of her wearing it. Her legs were bent toward her chest, with her arms wrapped around her knees.

"What's going on?" she asked, brows pulling together.

"Partial found at the Highland Path murder matches Caldwell's prints in the system. It's almost over, baby." At the mention of Calder, her body stiffened and she let out a forceful breath.

"But"—she shook her head—"that doesn't make any sense. He's not the man who took me. I'd know. He has to be sheltering someone." She clutched her knees more tightly. "How? How could he look at me every day and know? Smile at me?"

He hated Calder even more for putting that wounded look in her eyes. Of being one more person to let her down. Everyone at the barracks loved Calder. No one would've questioned his motives for being there.

"He always seemed so kind and warm. Sometimes, I'd ... I'd wonder if my life would be any different with a father so supportive and giving." A bitter chuff broke from her lips. "Instead, he's possibly involved in the most traumatic event in my life."

"We'll have answers soon." He opened his closet and yanked on pants and a shirt before rounding the bed. "You'll have justice. All those families will have peace." He leaned down and cupped her cheek. "About last night—"

Her eyes turned into slits, and she flinched away. "What about it?"

"Don't put those walls up. I just... Fuck. I can't protect you the way I need to when my head's so full of you I can't think straight. I want to do this right. We need to take a step back until all this shit is wrapped up. I'm relieved that seems like it will be sooner rather than later."

Hurt flashed over her features. "You regret it." Her voice was hollow, empty.

"I regret getting distracted when my sole focus should be keeping you safe. Don't mistake that with me not caring when you know damn well I do." Shit. He'd gone about this all wrong. Nothing good ever came after *about last night*. He couldn't be any more of an idiot.

"I can keep myself safe. What I can't deal with is you pulling away after what we shared. After I let myself be vulnerable for the first time ever. If you don't want this, fine, but don't use my situation—"

Easton slammed his mouth down on hers, effectively silencing her doubts. "Look at me. There's nothing I want more than to be with you. To do that, you need to be safe. Stay here. Please. I'll call as soon as I can. Keep the doors locked and the alarm set."

After a moment of hesitation, she nodded, and relief flooded through him. He'd smooth things out when all of this was over. She'd be safe in his home, even if he wasn't in it. He had to believe that or he'd never be able to focus on the task in front of him.

"Easton, I… Be safe, okay?" Her voice cracked. A silent plea flitted through her eyes, and his heart expanded in his chest.

"You too, Kins." He pressed his palms to her cheeks, momentarily blinded by emotion that had his heart hammering. When he turned to leave, an empty flutter tunneled through his stomach. He glanced over his shoulder before he closed the bedroom door behind him, savoring the sight of Kinley in his space. She'd be safe, and soon, she'd be free.

****

He met the other agents at the bureau's satellite office to brief before they drove to the residence on file at Lake Boone. Nothing but the dense forest was visible through the passenger side window of Agent Nilsson's SUV. Brigham and Dawson were bringing up the rear in the vehicle behind them, followed by their field Evidence Response Team. The tires jerked over the unpaved dirt drive, rolling over deep divots in the rocky terrain. Between the tree cover and the thick clouds tightly bound over the sky, it felt more like late afternoon than morning. Two miles off of the main road, they reached the address. The home was a two-story building that backed up against the water. An odd sensation prickled at the back of his neck—the kind he used to get when his mother explained in a voice void of emotion that one of her friends was coming over, and they were to do everything they were told.

The vehicle rolled to a stop, and he absently touched the weapon on his hip. This wasn't the first time he'd been in the field, but it was more typical for him to be at his desk, uncovering information. Before the other agents had arrived at the office, he'd hacked into Calder's computer. At first glance, nothing popped out to him as suspicious. Still, this was personal. He wanted to collect every scrap of technology in the house and transport it safely to the office, where he could dissect every bit of information on each device.

"Ready?" Nilsson asked, releasing her seatbelt.

He reached for the handle. "Let's go." The wind howled, and tree branches bowed. He fought to push the car door open, and the second he did, a raw gust snaked down the front of his black agency-issued tactical vest.

"We'll serve the arrest warrant," Dawson said. Easton had only spoken to the former Green Beret briefly in the past. The man's quick smile did nothing to detract from the lethal aura that surrounded him. "And take him in for questioning."

"This should've been a no-knock warrant," Nilsson bit out. "But he's friends with the judge who issued it."

"Let's get in there quick then, before he has the chance to destroy any evidence." If the judge thought that someone with ties to the Kingston Town Killer wouldn't be dangerous because of their status in the community, they were gravely mistaken. Easton wouldn't put it past the man to run or resist arrest.

Agent Brigham took the lead, walking purposely down the brick walkway toward the house. He didn't know her, but rumor had it she was fearless. With her dark eyes narrowed and shoulders squared, he could believe it. At the front door, she lifted her fist and pounded on the surface. "FBI. We're here to execute a warrant!"

Footsteps sounded from the inside before the door swung open. Maxwell Calder towered just beyond the frame. When he locked eyes on them, his posture stiffened. His lips curled in disgust. "What's going on here?"

"We have a warrant to search the property, and to bring you in for questioning regarding the murder of Becca Murray. You have the right to—"

He stepped onto the entryway, eyes bulging. "The murder of… Christ, this is ridiculous. Do you know who I am?" A forcible breath pushed past his lips. "Judge Hutchins would never allow this."

"I have two warrants that say otherwise, Mr. Calder." Brigham had skirted around him and cuffed his wrists. His face deepened to an ominous shade of red.

"I'll have your badges," he bit out, spit flying from the corners of his mouth. "Every one of you." He continued his verbal assault, voice rising as Brigham and Dawson led him to their vehicle.

With Calder out of the way, he and Nilsson cleared the house one room at a time, then spread out to search. Easton started with the downstairs office, boxing up the electronics. There was nothing of interest in the drawers or the wastebasket. He moved a stapler to the side to study a framed photograph of Calder and a young woman who shared no family resemblance. He remembered seeing her at the State Police Barracks working dispatch. Kinley would hate it, but the woman they all seemed so fond of needed to be questioned. The kitchen, bedrooms, and basement all revealed much of the same. Family photographs, knickknacks, and a child's drawings preserved in labeled boxes.

"Anything?" he called to Nilsson from the room

adjacent. Had someone tipped Calder off? There was nothing even remotely suspicious about the place so far.

"Just a bunch of creepy crawly stuff," she yelled back.

He paused, and his pulse kicked up a notch. "Frogs?"

"Err... Yeah, actually. Some snakes. A lizard." She stepped into the hall as he was coming toward her. "Take a look."

The room was about the size of the first-floor office. Terrariums of various sizes lined one wall. "Batrachotoxin," he muttered and peered in each tank.

"What?" Nilsson was at his side, looking like she'd rather be anywhere else than in the room they were standing in.

"The toxin used to kill the Becca Murray is found in Golden Dart Frogs. I'm no amphibian expert, but I think that little guy might be an accessory to murder."

She shook her head. "I don't think this case could get any stranger. I'll let the team know they're needed up here and fill Dawson and Brigham in on what we found," Nilsson muttered as she exited the room to notify the evidence response agents. "Maybe that will get Calder talking."

"I'll search the attic." He glanced up at the hatch door on the ceiling above and pulled the string to lower the fold-down staircase. The wood groaned beneath his weight as he tromped up to the top. He inhaled a quick breath and sneezed as layers of dust tickled his nose. An exposed lightbulb offered some visibility, but he took out his flashlight. The space was like any other attic. Cobwebs clung to exposed beams and worn boxes lined the corners and sides of the space.

He'd start with the boxes to his left and work his way around. The packing tape sealing the box was already peeling, and he stripped it off with ease. A child's drawings, report cards, and reports written in wobbly print made up the contents. He moved to the next. After an hour of searching, all he'd found were discarded toys, a coin collection, and old textbooks. The glint of something gold caught his eye, and he shoved the cardboard boxes aside to get a closer look. Suddenly, the temperature seemed to drop and the hair lifted on the back of his neck. An antique trunk was wedged behind the boxes. He looked over his shoulder, unable to shake the sense of dread tossing in his gut. He unlatched the trunk and lifted the lid. Beneath sheets of dust were albums and a few framed photographs. With tentative hands, he lifted the first picture of three children. On the far left was Maxwell Calder when he was young, a frown darkening his features. To the right was a boy of the same height. His posture was slightly stooped, and despite his wide grin, Easton found no warmth in the child's expression. Trapped between them was a little girl with pale hair and desperate eyes. His scalp prickled and he laid the picture to the side then grabbed an album. Breathing harder, he flipped through the pages of the book until he found what he was searching for. A different photograph of the three children. The yellowed corners had curled in, warping the image, but the cursive below was legible.

Max, Wayne, Janie - 1952

Janie. Those haunted eyes. The pieces were starting to come together, one sickening click at a time. Bile churned in his stomach. They'd just found the Kingston Town Killer's sixteenth victim—and his trigger.

Chapter Fifteen

Kinley parked beside Gus's patrol car and killed the engine. Easton was going to freak when he found out she'd left the house and that Gus had agreed she should come to the state police barracks. A member of the bureau had come to question Merry about her father and his ties to the Kingston Town Killer's case. There was a knock on her window, and she jumped, automatically reaching for her firearm. She put one hand over her racing heart and opened the car door.

"You scared the life out of me." Raindrops splashed against the car, carried by the unforgiving wind.

"Told you I'd walk you in," Gus said as they started toward the building. "Easton is going to lose his shit when he listens to the message I left him."

"You told him I was coming?" Her plan had been to get home before he did. *Home.* It was only a fantasy that she lived there right alongside Easton, but the last couple of days with him felt so unreal, it was easy to pretend.

"If my brother got home to find you gone, he'd burn down the state looking for you. Never seen him act like he does around you." Gus was speaking to her, but his eyes were scanning the parking lot as they rushed to the main doors.

"And how is that?" she asked, raising one brow. Her pulse was hammering, torn between wanting to know and being afraid the answer wouldn't be what she wanted to hear.

"Like a lovesick fool. Damn happy for you both." A smile ghosted his lips.

Her stomach dipped with pleasure even as her mind started protesting her partner's words. "He's keeping me safe. Working a case. When it's over—"

"Don't do that." His gaze sliced to hers. "I regret every moment I lost with Sasha in the beginning because I was questioning what I already knew. Had my head so far up my ass, I couldn't acknowledge what was right there in front of me."

"Well, she *was* the primary witness to our case." She grinned up at him and gave him a playful shoulder bump.

"Serious, Kinley." They stepped onto the sidewalk in front of the barracks, and Gus stopped. "If you don't see a future with him, cut him loose now."

"I didn't say I didn't." Her voice was a whisper, easily swept away with the wind and rain, but Gus nodded. "I'm scared."

"Get that, too." He placed a hand on her shoulder. "Easton won't let you down."

"That's not what I'm afraid of." She looked up at him, and his eyes softened.

"You won't let him down, either. If I thought you would, we would've talked long before now." Gus swung open the door to the barracks and gestured for her to walk in first.

"Enough with the feelings," she said, and Gus chuckled. "Why does Merry want me here so bad?"

"Agent Bryce just came from interviewing Maxwell Calder," he said as they passed the enclosed front desk. "Couldn't get a word out of him, so she's not making things easy for Merry. Showed her photographs of some of the Kingston Town Killer's vics." His tone hardened. They all had a soft spot for Merry.

"That's bullshit." She spat, quickening her pace down the corridor. "The more I thought about it last night, the more I'm sure she's innocent in all this. She's only twenty-two. Would have been five when I was taken."

"No one thinks she had a hand in any of it." They both veered to the right, making room for a trooper who was walking on the other side of the hall. "But could she know something? Possibly." Gus shrugged, and Kinley stormed into the interrogation room. The door slammed against the wall, startling Easton's boss.

Kinley paused as heat flushed through her. Merry was doubled over sobbing, and the metal table was littered with pictures. Ones she'd looked at a hundred times when she'd become obsessed with the case.

"Excuse me. I'm in the middle of interviewing—" the older woman began.

She shot her a warning glance, muscles quivering with anger, and crossed to Merry.

Kinley dropped to her knees beside her chair. "Breathe, honey."

Merry's gaze jerked up. Her eyes held more than just disgust or sadness from looking at the disturbing photos. This was something more. Something far worse.

"I-I...my heart. It hurts." Merry swayed forward, nearly collapsing off of the chair, and Kinley grabbed her shoulders to prevent her from falling. A sob was wrenched from her lips, a closed fist pressing into her sternum.

"What the hell happened?" She whirled on the agent behind her.

"She was handling it fine. Then I showed her the fifth victim." Bryce began collecting the photographs and placing them into a folder.

"What's in your hand, Merry?" For the first time, she noticed something crinkled in the dispatcher's closed fist. Merry's body shuddered, but she extended one quaking hand toward Kinley. With gentle fingers, she opened up Merry's hand.

She smoothed out the picture, and her heart thudded hard against her ribcage. "Oh, my God. Is this… Is—" Why hadn't she noticed the resemblance before now? Not just the large russet eyes with flecks of auburn or the thick black hair, but the shape of the women's bone structure. So similar, so perfectly aligned.

Merry nodded, tears streaming from eyes overripe with horror. Her hand went to her neck, clutching the locket she always wore. With an anguished scream, she yanked it, breaking the gold chain, and passed the piece of jewelry to Kinley. Her fingers quivered as she pried open the locket and sucked in a sharp breath. The crinkled photograph from the case file was a replica of the one inside Merry's locket. The fifth victim. The teenage daughter of two scientists who relocated with their company from Mumbai. She went missing two weeks after the family moved to Texas. Her charred remains were recovered nine months later.

"There was no car accident. My father didn't fall in love with a young woman on a business trip. She was a child!" Merry's voice broke, and Kinley wrapped her arms around her. They clung to each other, united by something so dark, she couldn't quite wrap her head around it. Merry's chest heaved as she fought to draw in a breath.

"Lambert," she barked, eyeballing Gus. "Get an EMT here. She's going into shock."

Gus lifted his phone and turned, speaking quietly into the device. Or maybe she just couldn't hear his words over Merry's cries and the ringing in her ears. "Is there anyone else in your family aside from you and your father?" She tried to meet the dispatcher's eyes, but they were downcast, and she refused to look up.

"Sorry. So…" Merry's voice cracked, and her fingers bit into Kinley's forearms. Only when the EMTs arrived and began checking her vitals did she reluctantly let go. Kinley moved out of the way of a paramedic and found Gus and Agent Bryce waiting outside.

"Conference room," Gus suggested, lifting his chin toward the room down the hall. They walked silently through the corridor, the only sound the scuff of shoes against the linoleum.

They entered the room, shutting the door behind them. Merry's locket was heavy in her hand, weighed down by lies and secrets. "Merry's father, Maxwell Calder, gave her this locket. Said her mother died in a car accident when she was very young."

"What do we know about the fifth victim?" Gus asked.

"Sana Das. Transplant from Mumbai. Two weeks after relocating, she disappeared. At sixteen, she was the oldest victim. He killed most of the girls after two or three months, but she was held for approximately nine months."

"And maybe now we know why." Gus rolled his shoulders with force.

"The fifth victim became pregnant. For whatever reason, the baby was kept alive and ended up with Maxwell Calder." Merry might have all the answers without knowing it—if the truth didn't kill her first.

"So, it's very likely that Calder is responsible for murdering those girls." A frown line ran down the center of Agent Bryce's forehead.

"It wasn't him. Maybe he was involved somehow. But he didn't rape and torture those children." The stained mattress. The stench of urine and blood, poorly masked by limestone. The steel chain staked into the dirt floor. Raw, festering boils from the manacle around her ankle. She could recall everything about those two months with agonizing detail. How had she survived it?

"How do you know?" Agent Bryce's tone was so dismissive, Kinley's body tensed and she gripped the edge of the table.

"I was there." She pushed away from the table and stalked out, leaving the door vibrating with the aftershocks of her anger.

Merry's connection to the killer. An innocent woman killed because she shared a likeness to Kinley. The possible involvement of a former FBI legend. All of the shit she'd been drowning in for the past weeks slammed into her chest. She tried to gulp down some of the stale barrack's air, but it wasn't enough. Not when she could hardly get oxygen past her tight throat. She rushed down the halls and burst from the building. Once she was far enough away from the front door, she slumped against the brick exterior and planted her hands on her knees. She consciously attempted to slow her breathing and get her heartrate under control. When the ground stopped rocking beneath her feet, she crossed the lot to her car. Hopefully, she'd make it home before Easton got back. She unlocked the doors and climbed into the driver's seat. The steering wheel was ice beneath the pads of her fingers, and late October felt more like January.

Shoot. She should've told Gus she was headed back to Easton's place, and she used the voice to text to send him a quick update. He'd understand. Not long ago, he'd been sucked into his own version of hell.

As she drove, Merry's shattered expression stuck in her mind. Was she really the daughter of the fifth victim? They'd be able to find out soon enough if Merry was willing to have a DNA test to verify paternity. A blur of green caught her eye in the rearview mirror. One of those tiny trucks was right on her bumper. What an asshole. She was about to make a rude gesture when unease spread through her. There was something familiar about the driver that made her cold all over.

The truck's tires squealed as it rammed into the side of her car at full speed, and the fear accompanied the cold. Stupid decisions led to people getting hurt, and leaving Easton's house, leaving the barracks alone, hadn't been her brightest idea. She picked up her phone, fingers poised over Easton's number, when the truck careened into her again. The device flew from her hands and thudded to the car floor. Her back tires spun out, and she cursed. Her heart was thrashing, and black spots blurred her vision. The huge oak tree seemed to come out of nowhere. The windshield splintered. Pain reverberated up her right ankle. The airbags deployed with a whoosh, blasting her in the solar plexus. The car careened down an embankment, rolling once. Tree bark flashed in her line of vision right before her temple struck the side window. There was the sickening crunch of bone, then nothing.

Chapter Sixteen

Easton stared into the eyes of Maxwell Calder and knew down to his bones they were missing something big.

"My client has nothing more to say, and you have no grounds to hold him." Calder's defense attorney, Isa Jagger, had shown up and stalled any forward progress. The woman had a reputation for being a pit bull in court, and she had gotten Judge Hutchins to expedite his detention hearing to later that afternoon.

"He's going to go down for first-degree murder in the death of Becca Murray. We have a trail that leads right to your client. Did he tell you Murray was an FBI informant during his days in South Boston?" He turned his attention to Calder. "What'd you promise her to lure her to the abandoned home on Highland Path?" He studied the man in silence, watching for any tells of deceit. He lifted his chin toward Jagger. "Maxwell dressed a dead woman to resemble the only survivor of the Kingston Town Killer, complete with a local newspaper from the year of her disappearance. Lived in the area at the time of the murders and moved to New England shortly after the surviving victim relocated up North."

Jagger narrowed her gaze across the table. "As you're well aware, you don't need to answer any questions, Mr. Calder," she said without sparing her client a glance. "These agents are grasping at straws. If you have nothing more to present, I'd like a private word with my client before the hearing."

"Actually." Agent Nilsson stood and smoothed her straight gray skirt. She picked up the old photo album and rounded the metal table and chairs. "We found something interesting at your residence." She laid down the photo album with the page open to the picture of three siblings. "When your brother Wayne killed Janie, did you help him cover it up?" Nilsson asked.

Calder recoiled at her words, eyes bulging.

Interesting.

"And when he raped her?" Easton added.

Calder's face blanched before heating to an intense shade of red. "I don't know what the hell you're playing at—"

"Mr. Calder. Not another word, please." Calder's attorney closed her leather-bound portfolio and quickly slid it into her bag on the floor.

"Wayne never touched her." The table jolted as Calder plowed his closed fists onto the metal and stood. "She died in her sleep, goddammit. Some undetected condition."

"Does telling yourself that help the guilt?" Nilsson leaned her hip against the side of the table, arms crossed over her chest.

Jagger's nostrils flared. "This meeting is over," she said with an air of finality.

"Janie was his first." Nilsson continued as though she hadn't heard Jagger's demand. "Maybe your brother didn't mean to kill her, but her death was the trigger. The reason he cut all the other girls' hair. No matter how many he took, they were never perfect. Not like Janie was."

"Come on, Mr. Calder." Jagger grabbed her client's arm and urged him toward the exit.

"Janie," Easton said, fighting to keep the disgust from his voice. "That's what he called those little girls as he was raping them, torturing them." What he'd called Kinley, dammit. "That's a classified detail, but maybe you've heard it. Did you know that, Mr. Calder? The fantasy never lived up to—"

The door slammed shut, cutting off his words, but right before it did, he'd seen what he was looking for.

Horror.

"If Judge Hutchins cuts him lose this afternoon, let's get a tail on Calder. He's going to go directly to Wayne." Soon, this would be over for Kinley. She wouldn't have to look over her shoulder at every turn. She'd be free to live her life. A life he hoped included him.

"He looked genuinely shocked by those allegations." Nilsson stepped back from the table. "He knew enough about the crimes to help Wayne evade arrest, but didn't know or didn't want to know what was going on underneath his own roof."

"No matter how evil someone is, it's hard to imagine your own blood turning on you." Just like his own mother had done. "I need to call Kinley and give her an update."

"I'm going to pull together some last-minute thoughts for the hearing. I'll be at my desk if you need me." Without waiting for his reply, she exited the back door of the interview room. Once the door closed, he immediately picked up his phone and dialed Kinley's number. It went right to voicemail. The hair on the back of his neck prickled, and he punched it in again.

Shit. Shit. Shit.

His heart thudded harder. He dialed the landline to his house, but the phone just rang. Kinley had no reason not to pick up or to have her phone turned off. Something was seriously wrong. He could feel it in the way his hands trembled as he punched in Gus's number. In the way his breathing had increased, along with sickness churning in his stomach.

The phone rang once before his brother's voice

boomed over the line. "Kinley fill you in?" Gus asked.

"Fill me in? She's not even picking up her phone." His voice wavered, and he didn't give a fuck. He was worried. There were so many things that could've gone wrong.

"Shit. She texted me a little over an hour ago to say she was headed back to your place." Phones were ringing in the background, and a police scanner relayed information to those on duty.

"Back? Christ, she was never supposed to leave." He stood, patting his pockets with frantic hands to locate his keys.

"Agent Bryce was fed up when she couldn't get anywhere with Calder, so she stormed down to the barracks and pulled his daughter in for questioning. After Bryce came down hard, Merry begged me to call Kinley." With each word, his brother's voice got harder. He wasn't the only one who thought something was terribly wrong.

"She should've called me. I never would've let her go alone. You should've fucking called me!" Not once in his life had he shouted at his brother, but he was hanging on to his sanity by a thread as he raced out of the field office into the damp October air. His shoes sponged over dead, waterlogged leaves as he ran and jumped into his temporary vehicle.

Gus let out a string of curses, none of them aimed at Easton. He was taking the weight of his screwup hard. "Wasn't thinking clear, but yeah, I should've. So damn sorry for letting you down, brother. We're going to find her. Where are you now?" The slam of a door and feet pounding over pavement were audible.

"Headed back to my place." He pulled out of the office parking lot on two wheels. "Maybe she did get to the house and fell asleep. I'm driving on the main roads.

You take the back. Get ahold of Isaac." He wanted her phone to be off for some logical reason. Maybe she'd forgotten to charge it when they were caught up in each other last night. Maybe she'd been in the shower and didn't hear the house phone ringing.

"Will do." Gus was beating himself up more than anyone else ever could, but at the moment, Easton had one focus. Getting to Kinley. What would he do if she disappeared? Imagining her hurt or in pain was a serrated blade slowly sinking beneath his skin. He wouldn't survive it. Kinley was the woman he thought he'd never find, and she was his. Now that he'd had her in his home, he couldn't picture the space empty of her goodness.

He hadn't even made it halfway home when he got an incoming call from Gus. "Where are you?" The tone of his brother's voice chilled his blood.

Easton's hands tightened on the wheel, blanching. "Just passed the pet store on route 495."

"Turn around." Gus was breathing hard like he'd just been running. "Found her car, Easton."

"Is she…" He trailed off, unable to say the words out loud. Sweat broke out on the small of his back.

"She's not here." His brother paused, the only sound his rapid breath. "Multiple tire tracks from the road. Her vehicle went over the embankment just past the golf course." Gus's voice was strained like he was holding back on something.

"Now's not the time to withhold information." Easton's vision narrowed, the physical pressure of Kinley missing crushing him. "What aren't you telling me?"

Gus cleared his throat and in a softer voice said, "Drag marks leading back to the road. Jules and Sasha are calling all the local hospitals. No one can get in touch with Isaac. He's out of the country on a mission."

"She's not at a hospital," he said with a growl. The Kingston Town Killer had stuck to crimes of opportunity until now.

"Know that. I also know Kinley's tough as hell." Gus was starting to sound as short of breath as Easton felt.

"He's got her. Fuck!" He slammed his fist into the steering wheel. "I promised nothing would touch her. That I'd protect her. Goddammit." His voice cracked.

"She'll hold on, Easton. She's strong. We'll get to her."

"When she's broken and bleeding?" The rage building inside him was going to detonate in three point two seconds. When it did, someone was going to get hurt whether they wanted to be in the crosshairs or not.

"Don't go there," Gus snapped. "You're no good to her like this."

He paused, trying to even out his ragged breath. Gus was right. He was doing her no favors by losing his shit. He needed to be numb and process the information of her disappearance just like he would at the bureau. He was damn good at what he did, but he'd never operated in a full-blown state of panic like he was right now.

"Needed that. Be there in ten." He hung up the line and clenched his teeth together. *Lock it down.* He got himself under control and then pulled down the side street next to Gus's state-issued vehicle. He parked and leaped from the SUV. Gus was standing at the edge of the embankment, and he ran up to meet him. Nothing could've prepared him for the pitch of revulsion in his gut as he stared down the steep, craggy hill. Shattered glass. Crumpled steel. One tire blown clean off of the car. But what had dread wriggling beneath his skin were the drag marks cutting a path through the dirt and brush, large, wide-set footprints on either side. The breath evaporated from his lungs, and he doubled over, bracing his quaking arms on his knees. A flash of heat tingled over his scalp, turning cold as the sensation slithered down his body.

Then Gus was at his side, hand clamped down on his shoulder in support. He straightened slowly and was dragged into a rough embrace. "I'll do anything to make this right." Gus's voice constricted.

"Then let's find her," he said. Gus stood at arm's length, one palm still on the back of his neck. No one would work harder to find Kinley. Not only because she was his brother's partner and friend, but because Easton loved her. He should've told her how he felt. Now he might never get that chance.

"Whatever you're thinking, shut it down," Gus said.

Two black vans were hauling ass up the street, and they screeched to a stop. The doors swung open and Nilsson jumped from the driver's seat, followed by Dawson, who exited the passenger side. Forensics began unloading from the van behind them, immediately starting to secure the scene. Flashing blue lights came next as three cruisers sped down the road, sirens blaring. Some of the tension eased from his shoulders. Gus had already called in the cavalry.

As Nilsson shouted orders, Dawson jogged up to them, acknowledging Gus with a chin lift. He placed his hand on Easton's shoulder, just as his brother had done. Gone was the ever-present grin, and his light eyes were hard. "We've got this, man. Go do what you do behind that computer screen and bring Wright home."

Dawson walked away, and he turned to Gus. "No fucking way I'm going back to my desk while everyone is out searching. We need to spread out. Need to—"

"Listen. If you were thinking clearly, if your

emotions weren't involved, you'd know you're her best chance of survival. You and I both know this dickwad is in the wind. Probably already has her holed up someplace that a search party would never stumble over. You're the only one who can pick up their trail."

Easton dragged his hands through his hair and tugged at the roots. "Kins is out there with a fucking monster. Doesn't feel right to go home."

"I get it, but there's no one better at uncovering information than you. If you're in the office, you won't be able to push boundaries like you can on your own system. I'm driving. Someone will come for your car. Need to fill you in on Merry, too." They ran to Gus's car, and he started the engine.

"What happened with Calder's daughter?" Easton flexed his fingers then balled his hands into fists.

"Don't think she's Calder's." Gus angled his chin toward Easton but looked right past him.

"Tell me." Everything inside him was scraped bare. Hallowed out like one of the jack-o-lanterns displayed on the porches they were whizzing past. He'd never felt so helpless.

"When Bryce was interviewing Merry, she showed her pictures of the victims." Gus exhaled a sharp breath. "The image of the fifth victim, who shares a serious likeness to Merry, was the same picture as the one in her locket. Calder gave it to her when she was young. Said her mom died in a car accident. Kinley is positive that Calder isn't the person who abducted her."

"His brother, Wayne." Fucking hell. He should've stayed planted in his house with Kinley until this shit was over, but he'd wanted to make it right for her. Wanted to be her hero and not just from behind his computer screen. In doing so, he'd left her vulnerable.

"Maxwell Calder has a brother?" Gus's gaze cut

over to him, then focused back on the road.

"Found a box of old photographs in his attic. There are numerous images of three siblings. The look in the sister's eyes…" He cleared his throat. "The pictures of the girl stop after 1955."

"You think Wayne killed her?" Gus held the wheel in a white-knuckled grip.

"I do." Easton rubbed his damp hands over his pants, his insides still turning, like his world was being torn from beneath his feet. "Maxwell confirmed she was dead, but he was adamant she passed in her sleep. When I mentioned Wayne called his victims by the sister's name, I saw something important."

"Doubt." Gus's lip curled in disgust.

He nodded. "Along with a healthy dose of horror. If that's what was happening, he didn't know." The closer they got to Easton's street, the more impatient he became.

"Or didn't want to know." Gus turned on his directional and turned right down the private drive.

"Exactly." He punched the garage door opener as they careened toward the house.

Gus cut the wheel, tires squealing against the slick road. The vehicle lurched to a stop in the garage. He reached above and absently pressed the remote to seal up the garage.

"Tell me what you need," Gus said from behind him as they rushed into the house.

"Get Merry on the line." He paced down the hall, dragging his hand through his hair. "She might know something without even realizing it. I want updates from the scene. I'm not playing by the book here. No time for additional warrants. I'll cover my tracks, but if you want to—"

"Don't insult me by asking that." His brother's

tone was clipped and pissed off. "I don't give two fucks what rules you break to get her back."

"Okay." He nodded, pain putting pressure on his chest. No matter what, his family was there for him.

For the next hour, Easton dredged up everything he could on Wayne Calder. Records from every school he'd ever attended, every doctor's visit, each run-in with the law. In the background, he was running a program of his own design, hacking into every satellite, traffic, and commercial security camera trying to get a hit on facial recognition.

"What'd you find?" Gus asked, pacing right outside the office door.

"Maxwell and Wayne were fraternal twins. Between the ages of seven and ten, there's a trail of paperwork on Wayne from school counselors, the pediatrician, and even some local police reports. Neighbor filed a complaint that his cat had been butchered and left on the doorstep. He'd told Wayne not to ride his bike on the lawn. Said he knew it was him because the boy was always catching and killing squirrels in his backyard. When he was nine, he got expelled from school for setting a fire in the girls' bathroom. Later that year, his mother took him to the doctor for repeated bedwetting. After that, all three Calder siblings were pulled out of the public school system. The pediatrician noted that the boy had old wounds and bruises and was concerned about the stability of the home. Nothing was done, though, until Janie's death was declared suspicious. Still, neither of the surviving children were ever removed."

Gus rubbed his hand down over his chin. "I haven't been able to get Merry on the phone. Left her several messages."

Easton's computer chimed with a new

notification. He jerked his chair toward the monitor. "Got something. Facial recognition at the scene. Accuracy is sixty percent because of the driver's position, but it's something. Another camera shows the same vehicle in westbound traffic. Tell Nilsson we're looking for a compact truck. A green Chevy S-10."

"Those were discontinued a hell of a long time ago," Gus responded, looking down at his phone.

"Hopefully that means it's not hard to find." *Please let them find it.*

"Calling now." Gus stalked out of the room, and Easton went back to searching.

With the multitude of residential and commercial cameras in the area, the truck was easy to track. The trail became more sporadic as the truck got out of the suburbs and into more rural areas. He lost the trail completely in Brookfield.

"Easton!" Gus bolted into his office, phone outstretched. "Merry Calder."

He grabbed the phone, heart pounding in his ears. "Easton," he choked out.

"Oh, God." A woman's pained voice broke over the line. "This is all my fault. I wanted her at the station. I-I—"

"Stop. Please stop," he barked, and she went silent. "I don't need your guilt," he said more gently. "We're all feeling it hard. I need your help."

"Anything," she sobbed.

"Your ... ah ... Maxwell Calder owns the property on Lake Boone. Does he own any other properties listed under different names? Maybe a business or—"

There was a fast intake of breath. "An LLC?"

"Yes." He tucked the phone between his ear and shoulder and prepared to type down the information

Merry relayed.

"Jane Elyse, LLC. Kinley asked me if there was anyone else in my family, but I couldn't answer her. I grew up with my alleged father and Uncle Wayne. Did my dad—uh, Maxwell murder those girls in Kingston?" Her voice wobbled. She was trying to hold herself together for his Kinley.

"We're going to find out. Thank you," he said. They'd just gotten a step closer. Goddamn, they were going to scour the property, turn over every rock and blade of grass.

"Wait," Merry yelled.

"What is it?" Time was ticking. He needed to move. Now.

"I just remembered, my dad always used to tell me that if something went wrong when he was undercover we'd go to the bunker he kept on that property, and it would be safe. He wrote the coordinates on the back of a framed painting in my apartment." Merry rattled off her apartment complex and promised one of her neighbors would be there to open the door. She was still under observation at the hospital. He didn't interrupt her to tell her it was unnecessary, that he was holding the address in his hands already. He released a long, pent-up breath. When that bastard had taken his woman underground, he'd dug his own grave. He just prayed Kins survived it.

After they updated the bureau and the state police, Gus insisted on taking the wheel again. He didn't want to admit it, but it was a good thing. He was out of his mind. Traffic was congested, and as the car inched along at an infuriating pace, Easton was ready to lose it. His control was slipping. Coldness pressed against the glass windows. The temperature had dropped, and his beautiful Kinley was somewhere out there. He'd been brave for a great many things, but losing Kinley struck his heart with a fear so deep it threatened to swallow him whole. If she… God—he couldn't even go there. If something happened to her, there would be a gaping chasm in his soul. He promised to protect her, and he'd failed. He wouldn't blame her for walking away from him when this was all said and done. How could he possibly deserve her when he'd fucked up so badly?

"Take a breath so you don't have a fuckin' stroke," Gus said as he cut the wheel to the right and broke several traffic laws. Thank Christ, they were finally moving.

"Told her I had her back," he choked out.

"And you have. You will." The closer they got to the address, the more Gus's features hardened. He was locking his feelings down in a way Easton couldn't. Not when it was Kinley. Not when he knew what she'd gone through at the killer's hands once already. "When we get there, we have to assess the situation. I know you're going crazy, but if you run in halfcocked, you're going to get us all killed."

"No fucking chance I'm waiting for backup. All the things he could be doing—" Fear clawed its way up his throat, making it hard to speak.

"Don't go there." Gus's gaze sliced over to him. "If he has her, if they are both in our sights, you need to go to Kinley. She's gonna need you, and I doubt you can be objective right now." Flakes of snow began to whip around the vehicle. Snow could cover tracks and reduce the chance of surviving overnight exposed to the elements.

"He deserves to die." Never had he gotten a rush of pleasure at the idea of killing someone, but he wanted to pummel the Kingston Town Killer until there was nothing left.

"Don't disagree. But he needs to be the one behind bars, not you." Gus slowed the car and took the exit ramp. They didn't stop in the small town, just drove straight through to the outskirts. Dirt roads replaced cracked pavement. Gone was the occasional house. Just spindly trees casting dark shadows over the rudimentary path. Somewhere close, Kinley was being held against her will, and there was nothing he wouldn't give to get her back unharmed.

"Stop." Easton held his hand out. "We're half a mile out. Let's leave the car and go on foot. I don't want to give him reasons to make a rash decision."

Gus nodded and pulled his car as close to the tree line as he could. Without another word, he turned off the engine and pocketed the key before rounding the hood and joining him on the other side. With cautious steps, they made their way through the forest. Every time a twig snapped beneath his boots, his heart froze. They were so close to finding her, but with each second that ticked by, each noise they made had the potential to alert someone to their presence. When the ramshackle hunting cabin came into view, the urge to rush in coursed through him. Gus had been right though. Now was not the time to go in guns blazing. At least not before they determined that no other victims were being held. They crept closer to the property, hidden by poorly maintained brush and weeds.

"Cabin looks dark." Blood roared in his ears. If they were too late or had come to the wrong location, it would cost Kinley her life.

His brother said nothing, but the weight of Gus's hand was suddenly present on his shoulder. "Brace," Gus said, squeezing his arm tighter.

Easton followed his gaze, and his stomach lurched. Bile seared a path up his throat. A hundred feet away, a portly man with stringy hair was coming around the side of the cabin, hands coated in blood.

Easton surged to his feet. His actions were governed by blind fury as he pounded across the brittle earth. Gus's shouts were a muffled sound he refused to process. There was only one thing on his mind, and that was eliminating the threat against his woman. The blood, possibly Kinley's, snapped through the last of his control. Red-hot hatred infiltrated his peripheral vision. The man had stopped in his tracks, his hollow eyes shifting from left to right, seeking an escape. Easton slammed into him, knocking them both to the hard ground. He raised his fist and pounded his fleshy cheek.

"You motherfucker," he seethed. "Where is she?"

The sick bastard's lips curved into a delighted smile.

"I'll gut you. I'll fucking gut you." Easton didn't recall moving, but he saw his hand in motion, punching the man over and over until the smirk was merely a pool of blood and broken teeth.

Gus barked his name. "Enough. We have to find Kinley." His brother shouldered him back and flipped the man on his stomach before pulling a pair of cuffs from his pocket. They left the bastard moaning on the ground and followed the tracks he left through the snow. Droplets of blood were apparent now, and only a few feet in front of him, a steel hatch was visible.

"Take one side," Easton said to Gus, and together, they pried open the top. Gus shone his light into the hole and caught sight of something beneath the bright stream.

Nothing could've prepared him. Nothing.

Chapter Seventeen

Kinley fought to suppress a whimper as a metallic echo scraped overhead. Her left temple throbbed, and her arms were so numb that they didn't feel attached to her body. She'd always known he'd find her eventually. Hoped and prayed that his milky blue eyes wouldn't be the last thing she saw. Maybe it was a blessing that one eye was swollen completely shut. She could see out of her right, but her vision was blurry at best. She was being held in some kind of sparse decontamination room with a primitive shower and a drain just in front of her bare feet.

When she came to the first time, she'd been quaking with cold, dressed only in her bra and underwear. The grinding of old metal sounded again, and filth fell like ash over her body. The hatch above opened, and she recoiled from the faint stream of light. The pain in her head was so extraordinary, moisture welled behind her lids. The left side of her face pulsed as tears tried to force their way through the swelling. Metal squealed as her captor climbed down a steel ladder, his muddy boots descending toward her. Her heartbeat was thready and far too fast. *Calm down.* At this rate, she'd go into cardiac arrest before finding a way out of this.

"I've dreamed of this."

That voice. That horrid voice had starred in her worst nightmares, and suddenly, all thoughts of fighting her captivity fled. The high-pitched whine broke something inside her, and she started to sob. There was no escaping this. Easton and Gus probably didn't even realize she was missing yet, although she had no idea how long she'd been out. Long enough for the blood to dry on her face, plastering her hair to the side of her temple and cheek. Each time she breathed, the tight skin pinched and pulled. She had to keep him talking. The alternative was her being in some kind of excruciating pain. "The fifth victim. Sana Das. Meredith Calder is her child, isn't she?"

The man looming above her sneered. "She was older than I thought. Bitch got pregnant."

"Why did she think your brother was her father?" Each word tasted vile on her tongue. "Did you ever tell her it was you?" Her voice was white-hot and spewing with decades of hate. "That you raped and killed her young mother?"

His foot flew into her hip, sending shockwaves rippling through her. "Quiet! If it were up to me, I would've killed her the second I found out, but Max said no. He was always saying fucking no! Wanted to keep the baby. Wanted to raise her as his own. Never what I want! Wouldn't let me near her." Spit drippled from his mouth, chest heaving.

Thank God for that. Merry had been spared this man's poison.

"I knew I'd find you again. Do you remember how you escaped?" A horrible smile stretched over plump, ruddy cheeks. His gut jutted out, testing the buttons of his shirt and revealing his pocked underbelly.

She wanted to tell him to go to hell, but her voice was paralyzed with fear. He patted the pocket of his filthy sweatpants, and right then and there, she wished for death. She didn't consider herself weak, but she'd been strong enough to endure his torture the first time and knew with intimate detail the cruelty in store for her. A dull silver object swayed in her line of vision, and terror snaked over her bare skin. A hammer was hooked to his pocket. "I see you remember. It's the same one."

Before she had time to flinch, he'd gripped the handle and brought the tool down on her shin bone. Stars exploded behind her lids as the bone snapped and shifted. Searing pain radiated up her legs and into her thighs. *Someone help me.*

He raised it high over his again, poised to strike. "No, please. No more," she sputtered as he slammed it into her other knee. She fell back and rolled to the side, unable to breathe, unable to think of anything but pain.

"Not gonna escape this time. We're going to have a lot more fun before I let you die." He stepped over her and jerked the tap. The shock of ice water beating down made every muscle constrict. The separated fragments of bone in her leg and knee screamed. Panic drove through her as water clogged her nose and throat. Breathless jerks wracked her body.

Help! The hollow space echoed with the drum of water and shrill, manic laughter. When the water abruptly turned off, she was gagging and shaking uncontrollably. Everything hurt, and the cold penetrated her body so deeply she wanted to shed her own skin to escape it. Without another word, he climbed slowly to the top of the ladder. Steel scraping steel as the hatch door opened was a torture all its own, and when a gust of autumn air rushed into the space and coated her freezing body, a cry of rage built in her throat, turning to a meager squeak as it passed her lips.

Blessed darkness began to swallow her. Why was this happening to her? Wasn't enduring this horror once enough? *Let me die. Please, please.*

When she stirred, the darkness still surrounded her. If she was in some kind of doomsday shelter, it made sense, but at some point, there had been light in the space. Maybe her vision had failed. She no longer felt pain or cold, and while it was so much better than the alternative, she knew she was dying. Temperatures were too cold outside, and combined with the freezing water, she'd be lucky to make it another few hours. Her body had lost too much heat and couldn't replace it nearly fast enough. She could no longer tell if she was shivering. Closing her eyes, she pictured Easton. Dark eyes that snapped with hunger when he looked at her. The same eyes that softened when he kissed her so gently like she was something precious. If she concentrated hard enough, she could feel his soft hair between her fingertips, just long enough to plunge her hands into. She loved the deep timbre of his voice. The odds he'd defied to become the man he was. Good to the core despite a torturous upbringing. It was at that moment that she realized what he'd given her.

Everything.

In the short span of a week, Easton had cared for her, protected her in a way that gave her a deep sense of peace, and offered his friendship. Had shared his family with her. His love. He hadn't said the words, but she recognized the emotion filling up his gaze when he was inside her. She hoped he saw it reflected in her eyes as well. She loved him. A profound, irrevocable emotion. Her only regret was not finding him sooner. Fighting her feelings for him and wasting time when she could've been wrapped up in him. Of not being able to hold him when something was weighing heavy on his shoulders. Of not sharing more smiles and laughter. The whole time they'd been together, it had been him giving everything. Holding on tight so she didn't break apart. She wanted to be there for him, too. Wanted to be a patch sewn on the quilt of his family.

The thud of feet tromping over hollow earth made her throat tighten. How far down did the numbness go? Would she feel it this time when he hurt her? The hatch opened, and the strobe of a flashlight illuminated the space.

"Fuck! Oh, fuck. She's here. Gus, she's in bad shape. She's…"

She'd never hear Easton sound so broken. Easton! Her heart would break if her mind was playing tricks on her. There was a thud, and the stomp of feet.

"Oh, God, baby. I'm so fucking sorry."

Inside, she was screaming with joy, but she couldn't get her body to respond. She was able to see him, hear him, but her brain and body were on lockdown. She was trapped inside herself, unable to do anything to aid in her rescue. There was another thud behind her.

"Wrap her in this. Did you get a pulse?" Gus's voice was thick and pained.

"Weak, but it's there," Easton choked out.

"Our girl is strong. Paramedics are going to lower down a backboard. Calder is in custody." Their voices drifted in and out. As long as she could hear them, she'd be safe.

"We're going to cut the ties binding your wrists, baby," Easton said. "Kills me, but it's going to hurt once the blood starts circulating. Just know a paramedic is climbing down now with morphine. I won't let you feel any more pain."

She felt her arms release, but with nothing but numbness, so limp, Easton and Gus had to position each appendage to shift her onto the stiff board. Something popped in the distance, but she was safe. Easton was here.

"What was that?" Gus's tone should've alarmed her, but she was so tired. A commotion above registered somewhere in her brain, but this time, she didn't have to wish for darkness to pull her under, it swallowed her whole.

Chapter Eighteen

Easton clutched Kinley's limp hand, running his thumb over her cool skin. He hadn't moved from his chair at her bedside, terrified she'd slip away from him. Sunlight filtered through the slats in the blinds of her hospital room. The memory of opening that steel hatch of that hellish bunker to find Kinley's body crumpled on the floor was acid in his veins. His heart had stopped beating, paralyzed with fear. Then he couldn't move fast enough. Didn't even bother with the ladder. Her weak pulse fluttering against the pads of his fingers was a sensation he'd never forget.

Both her legs were swollen and casted. Her body was bloodied and bruised, the skin marbled and cold to the touch. He couldn't think of the reasons she was nearly naked, but the doctor said there was no bruising consistent with sexual assault. He hoped she'd been spared that pain, but if not, he'd be there to help her work through it. The important thing was that she'd survived and he wouldn't take that for granted. Never.

"No shame in taking a breather. Or a nap," Isaac said in a hushed tone as he entered the hospital room. "Coffee." A large to-go cup was placed in his free hand. "Doughnuts," Isaac added, placing a paper bag on the hospital table next to him. "Never seen someone in more need of a sugar rush." His brother had returned from deployment the night Kinley disappeared and had taken a direct flight to Boston. Easton thought he couldn't have any more love for his fraternal twin, but once again, Isaac moved heaven and earth to be there for his family when they needed him most. "How's she doing?"

"Doctor was happy with her recovery during rounds this morning. She's been in and out, mumbling mostly. She's still on enough pain meds to take down a horse, so I get it." As soon as Kinley had been stabilized, she'd gone into surgery for the severe fractures to her leg and knee. Every sigh she made was his salvation. The ebb and flow of her pulse on the overhead monitor was the glue holding him together.

"She's one hell of a survivor. Looked pure evil in the eyes twice and pulled through. Perfect for you. You going to hop on the wedding train with Gus and Sasha?" Isaac dragged up a chair and sat beside him, his own coffee clutched in his hand.

"Not going to wait to get a ring on her finger." And he wouldn't.

Isaac nodded. "Pleased as hell for you, brother." He glanced away, and Easton was sure he saw something cloud his twin's expression, but it was gone just as quickly as it came.

"The way we're dropping like flies, you'll be next. Or Jules." His statement was meant as a joke, but an honest-to-God growl rumbled in Isaac's throat. So he hadn't imagined the strange look on his face. Pushing Isaac never got him anywhere. He'd talk when he was ready. Not once had his brother even mentioned a woman, but maybe somewhere along the line, he'd been burned.

"Anything on Maxwell Calder?" Isaac asked, changing the subject.

"Awaiting his detention hearing, and this time, the judge isn't expediting anything." Easton rubbed his hands over his eyes. He was bone-tired, but he'd never be able to sleep. Not until Kinley was home and in his arms.

"What a cluster." Isaac shook his head. "Judge releases him from federal custody and he goes directly to his brother and shoots him point-blank. They were twins, too. Arguably went through less trauma than we did. One turned into a serial killer. The other an accomplice."

"Guess you never know when genetics and environment make that perfect storm. Can't say I'm sorry Wayne is dead. He deserved it slow and painful. Deserved to look all those families whose lives he tore apart in the eyes. He's not coming back, though. No chance of escape six feet under. I'll take some comfort in that."

"He's dead?"

Both men jolted. The small, hoarse voice from the hospital bed was the best sound in the world. She'd awakened a few times, but only briefly, and this was her first pointed question about what had happened.

"Yeah, Kins. It's over." Tears burned behind his eyes. God, she was strong. "When we were getting you medical care, shots were fired. Judge Hutchins had approved bail for Maxwell Calder, and he went straight to Wayne and shot him. I think once he put the pieces together about the death of their sister Janie, he couldn't stop himself."

"A sister. Oh, my God. The poor thing." Her already pale face blanched, and he squeezed her hand in support.

"Sixteen victims," Isaac murmured.

"Maxwell admitted to everything," Easton told her. "When he discovered Wayne had sent you an email, he panicked and tried to scare you away. He murdered Becca Murray as a warning, thinking you'd run scared and not pursue the origin of the email. When that failed, he paid off Marshall Redding, the guard from Oasis Renewable Energy, to trash your apartment. He killed him, afraid he'd snitch to being recruited by Maxwell."

"Merry?" she croaked.

"Wayne's biological daughter. Maxwell could

only stomach so much. Apparently, killing a baby extended past his moral compass, so he kept her. Wayne was obsessed with you, and promised his brother he'd stop killing if they could relocate so he could keep an eye on you."

"Maxwell knew it was me all along." A single tear tracked down her cheek, and his heart squeezed. She was alive.

"Yeah, baby. He did. All the victims' families have been notified. Merry stopped by yesterday with flowers. Sana Das's parents have already contacted her. They want to meet their granddaughter, despite the circumstances surrounding her birth."

"Love that for her." Another tear fell.

"Me too. If it wasn't for her information…"

"Don't think about that," Isaac interrupted. "Just focus on the now."

Kinley's eyebrows rose, as if she just recognized that his brother was in the room.

"We met briefly during the crisis with Gus's fiancée. I'm Easton's brother. I'm sure you both have things you want to talk about." Isaac stood up and looked down at Kinley, warmth softening his hard features. "Glad to see you're okay, sweetheart. I'll bring Julie up tomorrow for a bit so you're not bored to tears."

"Thank you, Isaac."

"No. Thank you for being tough as hell and hanging on. Worked with seasoned SEALs who cracked under less. Let Easton take care of you." He slipped out of the room, and Easton turned his attention to Kinley. His entire world lay in that hospital bed.

"I love you, Kinley. So damn much. When I thought I'd never get the chance to tell you, it gutted me. I'm so sorry I didn't protect you better. I made a promise to keep you safe. I failed, and I almost lost you as a result. I will never take a single breath from your lungs for granted. You need to know that I'm going to do everything in my power to convince you to move into my home. Someday soon wear my ring." He feathered his hand over her hair, barely touching her but needing that contact. She was here. Breathing. His. "You are everything good and strong and beautiful. Maybe I'm being selfish and laying too much out there, but Kins, baby, I know. Always thought I wasn't able to connect with someone because of my past experiences. That I didn't have it in me to love because I was too broken. Turns out, I was just waiting for you. Waiting for you to teach me that love is the glue to mend those shattered pieces. That the cracks and breaks don't make me weak or untouchable. Each one represents a trauma, and each one has given me something in return. Empathy. Courage. The knowledge that I want to be someone who lifts others up, not tears them down. And I learned that because I see every beautiful broken piece in you, and it takes my breath."

Tears shimmered in the beautiful golden depths of her eyes. She squeezed his hand, and even though her grip was still weak, it was another sign that she was healing. "My only regret when I was in that bunker was not having a chance to tell you how I feel." Every emotion was clear on her face, but the one that shone through the most was love.

They'd both fallen. He didn't need the words he suspected were coming, but damn, he hoped to hear them.

"That in two short weeks you gave me everything. You protected me and welcomed me into your home. Shared your friendship and family. Your love. Everything, Easton. And don't you dare shoulder any guilt—you saved my life." She stopped to catch her breath.

"Rest, Kins. Get your strength back. We have all the time in the world to talk about this. I'm not going anywhere." God, she was strong.

She shook her head. His woman was stubborn, too.

She took a raspy breath. "I was the one to leave and drive alone to the barracks. I was the one who took off on Gus. Stupid decisions that I regret, but what I'm not sorry for is the new beginning we've been given." She paused again, but this time he didn't interrupt her. "You freed me from Calder. If I had died, it would've been with the knowledge that you'd made my life so rich in such a short time. I love you, Easton, and you're not going to have to push. The only place I want to be is with you."

His throat was tight, and there was a burn behind his eyelids. She said he gave her everything, and he'd spend the rest of his days proving she was everything. "You'll come home with me? Our home?"

"Yes." A glorious smile tipped the corners of her lips.

"I love you," he said, leaning forward and peppering her face with gentle kisses. Her hoarse laughter filled the room, and his heart.

"And I love you. Prepare to be showered in it every day for the rest of your life," she said, lashed fluttering shut.

"Can't wait, baby," he murmured.

Kinley's pain meds were making her drift off again, but this time, her expression was relaxed. Peaceful. Happy. All the feelings expanded in his chest, making his heart soar.

"Me neither, Easton."

Epilogue

Kinley closed her eyes for a moment, soaking in all of the joy and chaos. Nutmeg and cinnamon swirled in the air from the pumpkin pie she'd helped bake and set on the counter to cool. Easton was at her side, their linked hands resting on the table that was lined with so much delicious food her stomach grumbled. Their entire family was gathered. Gus, Sasha, Julie, and Isaac were all seated in the dining room. Two puppies, Gunner and Echo, wrestled on the floor at their feet, playing while waiting for some Thanksgiving scraps. Every so often, they'd bounce too close to Gilligan, shaking a growl loose from the old dog, and the pups would bolt with their tails tucked. Once she'd been freed from her casts, they'd gone to a local shelter and welcomed the pair home. The silly fur balls added even more love and laughter to their household.

Later, Merry, Lena, Tyler, and Eliza were joining them for dessert. The people who had aided in her rescue became fast friends. Jules had passed her exams and was working as an in-home therapist for kids of all abilities. To celebrate her achievements, they'd done Julie's favorite thing and cozied up in the Adirondack chairs on the outdoor patio at Gus's house. The warmth from the stacked stone hearth had chased away the November chill while they roasted marshmallows for s'mores. She'd worn the delicate platinum bracelet with a jeweled puzzle piece they'd all chipped in for and gifted her.

Easton hadn't wasted time proposing to Kinley. The morning after she'd returned from the hospital, they'd been snuggled in bed, enjoying being alive and together when he'd rolled to his side and removed a black box from his nightstand. Bathed in warm light from sunrise, Easton slipped the diamond on her finger, the round stone casting rainbows around the room. She loved the way her heart expanded when his unbridled smile hit her at full force, or his growing sense of humor. She had everything.

Everything she could ever want. Everything she could ever need.

The End

CHARLEE JAMES

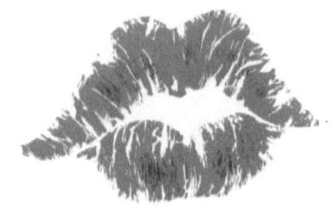

EVERNIGHT PUBLISHING ®

www.evernightpublishing.com